Dog Is in the Details
a golden retriever mystery

Neil S. Plakcy

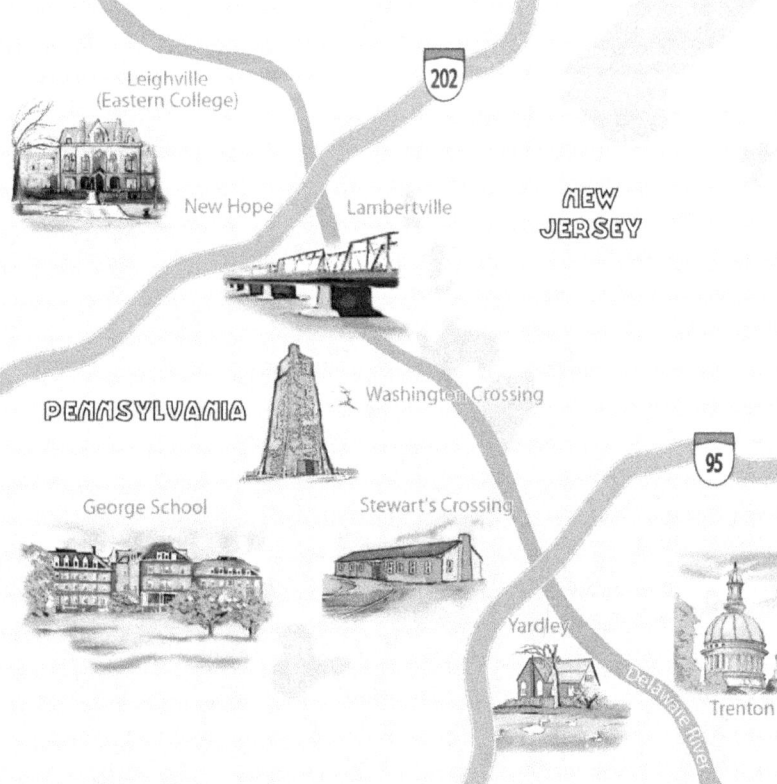

Copyright 2017 Neil S. Plakcy. All rights reserved, including the right of reproduction in whole or in part in any form.

This book is a work of fiction. Names, characters, places, and incidents either are products of the author's imagination or are used fictitiously. Any resemblance to actual events or locales or persons, living or dead, is entirely coincidental.

Reviews

Mr. Plakcy did a terrific job in this cozy mystery. He has a smooth writing style that kept the story flowing evenly. The dialogue and descriptions were right on target.

Red Adept

Steve and Rochester become quite a team and Neil Plakcy is the kind of writer that I want to tell me this story. It's a fun read which will keep you turning pages very quickly.

Amos Lassen – *Amazon top 100 reviewer Amos Lassen*

We who love our dogs know that they are wiser than we are, and Plakcy captures that feeling perfectly with the relationship between Steve and Rochester.

Christine Kling, author of *Circle of Bones*

In Dog We Trust is a very well-crafted mystery that kept me guessing up until Steve figured out where things were going.

E-book addict reviews

Chapter 1
Handsome Boy

The field beside the synagogue, used for overflow High Holy Day parking, was filled with enough dogs, cats, hamsters and other animals to populate an ark. My golden retriever Rochester strained at his leash to go play and I struggled to hold him back.

"I had no idea there would be so many people and dogs here," I said to Lili.

"They all want their pets to be blessed." She reached down and scratched behind the golden's ears. "You want your blessing, don't you, boy?"

As Rochester woofed in agreement, I looked at Dr. Liliana Weinstock, chair of the Fine Arts department at Eastern College, where I worked as well, and marveled that she had chosen to share her life with me and Rochester. She was a beautiful woman in her mid-forties, three years older than I was, and nearly as tall as my six feet, with luxuriant auburn curls and a Cupid's bow mouth, one I was lucky to be able to kiss regularly.

A few days before, I'd gone to Shomrei Torah's website to check the times for the upcoming High Holy Day services. Sandwiched between the listings of bar and bat mitzvahs and information on the rabbi's Talmud study group I spotted an announcement that the temple was sponsoring a blessing of the animals that Sunday, and decided to take Rochester. Since he had a tendency to get into trouble, digging up clues that led to bringing criminals to justice, I figured we could use all the blessings available.

When I was growing up in Stewart's Crossing, Pennsylvania, there were few Jews in our neighborhood and no synagogues on our side of the Delaware River, just Catholic, Methodist and Presbyterian churches. So we had to travel into Trenton to worship.

Back then, our Reform congregation, Shomrei Torah, Guardians of the Torah, had been housed in a beautiful nineteenth- century stone building in central Trenton. Long after I'd had my bar mitzvah there, been confirmed and graduated from Hebrew High School, the congregation sold the building and moved out to this new temple on the Pennsylvania side of the river, in what had once been farmland alongside I-95, just a mile inland from the Scudder Falls bridge, and technically within the borough limits of Stewart's Crossing.

I had been to services there a couple of times before, on the Yahrzeit, or anniversary of the death, of my parents. The sanctuary was modern and lovely, with big glass windows that looked out on the nature preserve behind the building, but it wasn't the temple I'd grown up with and so I still felt like a relative stranger.

Lili, Rochester and I threaded our way toward the center of the field, where the rabbi stood with a beautiful female golden retriever by his side, past little girls cuddling hamsters, a woman with a Yorkie peeking out of a shoulder bag, families with cats in carriers and mixed-breed dogs on leashes.

Rochester whimpered and tugged, and I assumed it was because he wanted to play with Rabbi Goldberg's golden. The rabbi was in his late thirties, about a decade younger than I was, and he had a modern, welcoming demeanor, which I'd experienced those times I'd attended his services. That Sunday morning, he wore jeans and a polo shirt, with a white yarmulke and white sash around his shoulders.

Before we could reach him and his dog, though, a tall, broad-shouldered man standing beside him picked up a microphone attached to a portable amplifier and said, "Shalom, and welcome to Shomrei Torah on this beautiful September morning."

Several people in the audience called out, "Shalom!" and a couple of dogs barked.

The man laughed. He held a black miniature pinscher under his arm. "See, even our animal companions are glad to be here. And they're our focus this morning. My name is Aaron Feinberg, and I'm the president of our congregation. I'm delighted that Rabbi Goldberg has initiated this event, and I know Buster here is looking forward to his blessing."

One of the traditions of Shomrei Torah was that the Men's Club or the Sisterhood presented gifts to bar and bat mitzvah celebrants. Feinberg had been the president of the Men's Club when I turned thirteen, and he'd come up on the bema after I read from the Torah to present me with a silver-plated Kiddush cup and a Bible and prayer book embossed with my name. I still had the cup, but the Bible had been lost somewhere along my journey. Shomrei Torah had long since replaced the prayer book with a more updated one that no longer referred to God with male pronouns, and added Sarah, Rebecca, Rachel and Leah to the prayer to our fathers.

During my years away from Stewart's Crossing, Feinberg had kept up his involvement with Shomrei Torah, and was now in his third term as president of the congregation. He owned a furniture store with several outlets in the suburbs and busied himself with charitable works in the community as well.

The audience clapped lightly, and Rabbi Rob Goldberg took the mic. "Thank you, Aaron. It's a pleasure to have you all here. Before I get to the blessings, though, I'd like to tell you a little about their origin."

I heard the screech of air brakes as a big SEPTA bus pulled to a stop at the parking lot entrance. A rumpled-looking man with a backpack over his shoulder stepped down and looked around, then headed toward us. Because of his layers of clothing and his general air of dishabille, I had the impression he was homeless. As well, there was something vaguely menacing about the set of his shoulders.

Rabbi Goldberg's voice brought me back as he spoke about the first Chief Rabbi of the state of Israel, who envisioned our being able to share Torah with animals in the world to come. He spoke simply, as if he was particularly addressing the children in the audience.

"In Judaism, we perform a ceremony called a *hilula* on the anniversary of the death of an important teacher. Since the Chief Rabbi's *hilula* will be observed this Tuesday, my golden here, Sadie, and I thought it would be fitting to celebrate this blessing now."

A kitten in a little girl's arms mewed softly as the rabbi spread his arms out to encompass all of us in the field and began to pray. "*Baruch ata adonai.* Blessed are You, Holy One, Maker of all living creatures." He spoke in Hebrew and then in English, ending with, "Blessed are You, our God, whose spirit exists in all your creatures!"

He lowered his hands and said, "And let us all say, Amen."

The humans echoed him, and a couple of dogs barked. Then he began moving through the crowd, providing individual blessings to each animal. There was a happy, relaxed vibe in the field, so I was surprised when I heard raised voices coming from the parking lot.

The bearded man I thought might be homeless was arguing with the security guard who had been directing traffic. As I watched, the man broke away from the guard and strode toward the field, shouting something that sounded like, "I know what's going on!"

My immediate reaction was that I'd been right, the man had mental problems. Aaron Feinberg handed his little dog to his wife and moved to intercept the intruder. A moment later, two of Feinberg's elderly friends moved to join him.

Feinberg tried to put his arm around the bearded man's shoulder, presumably to steer him back to the street, and the man elbowed him hard in the stomach. Feinberg stumbled backward, and the other two men tried to strong-arm the man. The rest of the crowd seemed focused on the rabbi, and the security guard was out at the street entrance directing traffic.

Rochester jumped and wiggled, then suddenly slipped free of his collar and rushed toward the group. In the past, Rochester had attacked anyone who tried to hurt me, but I'd never seen him take off like this against a stranger who posed no threat to me.

I ran after him, calling his name, but his four legs moved faster than my two, and he was able to duck around people in a way I couldn't. Ahead of me, the bearded man had broken away from Benesch and Namias and faced them defiantly, his fists up. Feinberg stood hunched over beside them.

The crowd had cleared around the four of them, and Rochester galloped right into the mix. I assumed that he was going to try and knock down the bearded man, to protect Feinberg's friends, but I was wrong.

I was still a dozen feet away when Rochester raced to a stop in front of the bearded man, then sat on his hind legs. Instead of attacking the man, it looked like he was trying to protect him.

What if the man struck out at him? Could he hurt my beloved dog? I wouldn't stand for that.

Then the man's posture changed as he reached down and patted Rochester's head. Feinberg and his cronies looked surprised as the homeless man began speaking quietly to Rochester and scratching him beneath his chin.

"I'm so sorry," I said, apologizing to everyone for Rochester getting loose. "Rochester, come here!"

"It's all right," the homeless man said. "I love dogs. My brother has a golden retriever." He looked much calmer than he had when he arrived, though Feinberg and the others still looked skeptical.

Rabbi Goldberg arrived beside me with Sadie, and Rochester left his place in front of the man to nose the female.

"Joel," the rabbi said. "What are you doing here?"

Joel smiled, as if he wasn't aware of the chaos he'd caused. "I came to see you."

The rabbi took a deep breath and turned to those of us gathered in a circle around Feinberg, his friends, and the man named Joel. "Everything's fine," the rabbi said. "This is my brother, Joel."

I managed to get Rochester's collar around his neck again, and held tight to his leash. He was no longer straining to get away from me, though. The rabbi's golden, Sadie, had taken his place in front of Joel.

"I have to talk to you, Robbie," Joel said. "I have something to show you. It's about the Holocaust." He began to pull his backpack from his shoulder.

The rabbi held up his hand. "Why don't you wait in my office and I'll come join you as soon as I finish here."

Joel stopped, his backpack still on one shoulder. "Nana and Pop-Pop would want us to expose all the secrets. They didn't survive the camps just to let the Germans win."

"The Germans didn't win," the rabbi said softly. "You know that, Joel."

"But they're still here. They need to be punished!"

"Joel." The rabbi's voice was stern. "Take Sadie and go to my office."

Sadie jumped up at the mention of her name, and the rabbi handed Joel her leash. "Okay," Joel said, docile now. "Come with me, girl."

With typical golden retriever joy, Sadie accompanied Joel as he turned to walk toward the synagogue building. "It's around the back," the rabbi called after his brother. "There's an outside door that says Rabbi's Study. Sadie will lead you there."

After Joel was gone, the rabbi turned to Feinberg and the elderly men with him. All three men looked angry.

"I'm sorry, I didn't even know that my brother was in the area," Rabbi Goldberg said. "He has schizophrenia, and it's been very difficult to keep track of him. We mostly communicate through email."

"He shouldn't have come here like this," one of the men said. His name was Saul Benesch, and he had recently commemorated his eightieth birthday by purchasing a Torah salvaged from a congregation in Poland, paying for its restoration, and donating it to Shomrei Torah.

The other man was Henry Namias, and he and Benesch had been friends of Feinberg's father. They, and the elder Feinberg, had run Shomrei Torah all my life. "Is this the brother you had the problem with in Milwaukee?" Namias asked. "We asked you about him when we interviewed you."

"He wasn't a problem then and it won't be one now," Rabbi Goldberg said. "Joel just gets excited. He's not a danger to anyone."

"He certainly sounded like he was trouble," Benesch said, his voice quavering with age.

"My dog is a very good judge of character," I said, as Rochester sat at my side. "I'm sure he wouldn't have been so friendly toward Joel if he wasn't a good person."

Feinberg peered at me. "I know you, don't I?" "Steve Levitan. I was a bar mitzvah here."

He nodded. "I remember you. Weren't you the president of our youth group at one point?"

"Vice president. But that was a long time ago."

"Well, nice to have you back in the fold." Feinberg shook my hand, and I was pleased to have dissipated some of the tension in the group by speaking up.

Feinberg, Benesch and Namias walked away, their heads together and their voices low. The rabbi looked around us at the group of people and animals and said, "Well, I should get back to blessings. Who is this handsome boy?"

"Rochester."

"Thank you for coming today, and for helping out with my brother." It took me a second to realize he was speaking to the dog, not to me. Then he looked up. "Is there any special blessing you'd like for Rochester?"

I hesitated but then plunged in. "He has a nose for detection. He's gotten us in trouble a couple of times because he's found clues in murder cases."

The rabbi's eyebrows rose but he didn't say anything. "So a blessing to keep him safe would be nice," I said.

He leaned down and placed his hand flat on the top of Rochester's golden head. "*Adonai yiverecheka v'yishmerecha*. May the Holy One bless you and protect you." He stood up. "For a little extra blessing you can always bring him with you to my Talmud study group on Wednesday mornings. Sadie comes along, and I'm sure she'd welcome the company."

"I can bring a dog into the temple?"

"We meet in my study, and Rochester's always welcome there. And so are you. If you were a bar mitzvah here, I'm sure you already have a pretty good foundation in religious thought."

"Well, it was a long time ago, but I have been looking for something more spiritual in my life. Perhaps we'll join you one day."

Rabbi Goldberg shook my hand, petted Rochester, and then moved on to a huge St. Bernard. Rochester looked up at me, his mouth open in a doggy grin. He'd be happy to join the Talmud study group if he got to play with Sadie.

As we walked back toward where Lili waited for us, I saw Sadie leading Joel round the corner of the sanctuary building. The poor guy – he seemed to have lost his way. I had, too, though I hadn't been a victim of mental illness, and I'd been able to find my way back to happiness. There were a lot of ways to be lost.

I wondered what Joel Goldberg was so upset about. What did the Holocaust have to do with anything in the present day? And why had Feinberg and his cronies been so quick to intercept him?

Chapter 2
Difficult Decisions

When Rochester and I returned home from our walk that evening, I heard Lili's voice floating down from the second floor of the townhouse, and realized that she was speaking rapid, almost angry Spanish. While I knew that she'd grown up with the language, and that it still flavored her speech, I rarely heard her speak it with such fluency.

Her voice grew louder as she descended the stairs. *"Adiós, mamá. Te hablaré mañana."*

"Your mother?" I asked as she walked into the kitchen, her cell phone in her hand. I had taken out a big eggplant from the refrigerator and was ready to start preparing the eggplant parmigiana I'd learned to make from a vegetarian friend in college.

Lili sat on one of the Windsor-style kitchen chairs and nodded. "She's mad at my sister-in-law for the eighteenth time this week. I can't wait to hear Fedi's side of this one. They're really pressuring my mother to move in with them."

Lili's brother, his wife, and two children lived in Parkland, Florida, which I understood was about as far west of Fort Lauderdale as you could get without falling into the Everglades. Fedi had added a mother-in-law unit to his house, but their mother refused to leave her oceanfront apartment, even though she was having more and more difficulty living on her own.

"I can see why she doesn't want to move. It would be a big change for her," I said. "No more independence, no more living by the beach. She'd have to have someone drive her everywhere."

"I know. But change is inevitable and at some point she's going to have to get with the program." She sighed. "I have a feeling that the only way I'm going to make any impact with her is to see her in person."

Rochester crouched on the floor beside Lili, gnawing at his squeaky ball. "You could fly down for few days couldn't you?" I asked. As the chair of her department, Lili's role was primarily administrative, though she taught one class on Mondays.

She pried the squeaky ball from Rochester's jaw and tossed it toward the living room, and he took off after it. "I could. I have the vacation time, and the department can run without me for a few days. But I'm afraid my mother's problems run deeper than just giving up her apartment."

"Your family did move a lot. I can imagine it's hard to feel rooted."

"It can be. This apartment is the first place she chose herself, after my father died and she didn't have to follow him around. She's always loved the ocean and she was happy to find a building with lots of other Spanish speakers. She plays canasta with a bunch of Jewish women from South America and they do water aerobics in her pool in Spanish."

I had yet to meet Senora Weinstock, though I had spoken to her on the phone. "*Al fin un Judio,*" she had said to me in our initial conversation. At last, Lili had found a Jew. Lili had flown down to Florida a couple of times, always in the winter, to spend some time with her family, and always returned vaguely unhappy.

I understood what she felt. I loved living in Stewart's Crossing, relishing in the sense of rootedness that it gave me. My family had moved from Trenton when I was two years old, and I had grown up in Bucks County.

Back then, I'd been desperate, as many teenagers are, to escape the suburbs for the big city. After graduate school in New York I'd married and followed my wife to Silicon Valley so she could take a high-powered job. After Mary suffered her second miscarriage, I'd used my computer skills to hack into her credit records and set flags so that she couldn't run us into more debt. I'd been caught and punished, resulting in the end of my marriage and my return to Stewart's Crossing after a year in the California penal system.

I finished slicing the eggplant and began breading it as Rochester returned to the kitchen and danced around underfoot. "You do not eat eggplant," I said to him. "Go lay down, and I'll feed you your dinner soon."

I pointed to the puffy round bed in the corner of the breakfast nook, and Rochester slunk over there with his tail down as if he was being punished. "I am wise to your tricks, Mister," I said. "That sad look does not work."

He settled into the bed and looked up at me with a wide grin. I had inherited Rochester two years before, after the death of his previous owner, my next-door neighbor, and though it hadn't been love at first sight, eventually he had become the main reason I'd come back to life.

I'd come a long way since then, and I was grateful for all the blessings in my life. Now if Rochester could just keep from nosing into any crimes for a while, we'd all be able to settle in happily.

As I layered the sautéed eggplant with mozzarella cheese and tomato sauce, my brain started ticking. A year before, I'd been named the director of Eastern's Friar Lake Conference Center, responsible for creating and managing a regular series of executive education and alumni relations programs at a former abbey a few miles from the campus.

I'd put together a number of great events and more on the calendar, but I needed to start planning for the next year. Maybe I could put together a weekend program on the political, sociological, emotional and financial aspects of immigration

Once I had finished layering the breaded eggplant with mushrooms, tomato sauce and mozzarella cheese, I slid the casserole in the oven. I turned to Lili and told her what I was thinking. "You think people would be interested in a program like that? It would certainly be newsworthy, given the current political climate."

Lili looked up from her phone. "Do you know Andrea Del Presto in the sociology department? She's been doing a research project on twenty-first century migration and immigration. Maybe you could have her put together a program for you."

"I don't know her, but I've read about her research. We have a lot of first-generation American students at Eastern, as well as some who were born in other countries and grew up here. Many of my students are disturbed by all the anti-immigrant rhetoric you hear on the Internet these days."

"One of the young women in my Introduction to Photography class wears a hijab," Lili said. "She told us on the first day of class that she liked taking pictures because she could hide behind her camera. That she felt safer that way."

She shook her head. "That's so sad, that someone should feel they need to hide in this day and age."

"What do you call yourself if someone asks? Are you Jewish first, American first, Latina first? A hyphen of something?"

"It's hard to say. Ask me around Rosh Hashanah, and I'll say I'm Jewish first. Independence Day? American. When I talk to my family in Spanish I'd probably say Latina. I guess I'm a mix of all those. What about you?"

"I'm easier. Just Jewish and American. Hard to say which comes first because both of those identities are so ingrained in me. I wonder, though, what the next generation thinks."

"Sounds like something to ask next time you meet with them," Lili said. "But I'll bet they have the same trouble making distinctions."

I remembered Rabbi Goldberg's brother Joel, and his comments about the Holocaust, and how the Germans were among us. In Sunday School we'd spent a year studying the Holocaust, including articles about Nazi hunters who had devoted their lives to tracking down surviving members of Hitler's government, concentration camp guards and those who had ratted out their Jewish friends and neighbors.

Were any of those people still alive? If they were, they'd have to be in their eighties or nineties, and they'd had to live for decades with the guilt of what they'd done. Was there someone like that living among us? Or was I putting too much emphasis on Joel's statements? We finished dinner, and while Lili cleaned up I sat on the living room floor and played tug-a-rope with Rochester. I kept going back to the way he'd approached Joel Goldberg to protect him, wondering why.

Lili came into the living room, drying her hands on a cloth towel. "I'm probably going to have to go to Florida, you know. But I'm going to try and hold out until it gets colder here so it will seem like a vacation."

I mimicked surprise. "A vacation? From me?"

She pursed her lips as she sat down on the sofa. "From winter.

Though if you don't behave I may need a vacation from you, too." "I could misbehave." I reached up and tickled her foot. "Now that," she said, "is not a difficult decision to make."

Chapter 3
Close the Door

Monday morning, with Rochester by my side, I drove up the River Road from Stewart's Crossing to Friar Lake. Oaks and maples lined the winding road up the hill to the original stone buildings, and they were beginning to turn the reds, oranges and golds of fall.

As I pulled into the parking lot in front of the original slate-roofed gatehouse, which now served as my office, I looked around, as I often did, and marveled that I had been able to nurture the conversion of a run-down collection of buildings into a modern facility with meeting rooms, a dormitory and a kitchen, as well as acres of walking trails peppered by some older as yet unused outbuildings.

I had been stunned when Eastern's president offered me the job of converting, and then running the property, because I was a guy with an MA in English and little management experience as well as a convicted felon, still on parole.

He'd taken a big chance on me, and I was determined to prove I could do a good job. I'd worked my butt off during the renovation, and created a kick-ass series of programs. But every day I had to justify that faith by keeping the center going, continuing to engage faculty, alumni and students. It was a pressure I put on myself;

though the president was a demanding boss, he'd never criticized my commitment or my work.

I settled down in my office, which had a big picture window looking out on the property. Rochester plopped on his side next to my desk, and as I looked up Professor Andrea del Presto's information I heard him begin to snore gently.

I emailed her and was pleased that she responded quickly, agreeing to an appointment that afternoon to talk about a possible program at Friar Lake. I was still worried about the comment Joel Goldberg had made the day before, so I did some searching online for German survivors of the Holocaust. Perhaps there was a way to tie that into the program as well. The current administration had made a priority of denying admission to immigrants with criminal records, so there was definite connection to the prosecution of Nazi-era villains.

I found a website that listed nearly three dozen Germans and Poles on a list of those slated for possible prosecution for war crimes, including radio operators, medics and camp guards, as well as many listed as simply "participated in the murder of…" or "accessory to the murder of."

It was chilling. But many were believed to have died before prosecution, and the youngest listed was 91. Did Joel Goldberg suspect that someone on that list was living in Stewart's Crossing?

Or was his interest simply a manifestation of his schizophrenia? There was certainly a lot of anti-immigrant sentiment in the air around us, and it was possible that he'd internalized that and connected it to whatever he'd learned from his grandparents about the Holocaust.

After a while I couldn't read anymore. One of the reasons I'd taken the job was that Rochester could come with me, and he loved the chance to romp around the property and through the adjacent woods in search of interesting smells and squirrels and field mice to chase. So I took him out for a long walk in the fresh air. We ended up sitting at a picnic table beneath a majestic maple, sharing the roast beef sandwich I'd prepared for myself for lunch.

After we finished eating I sought out Joey Capodilupo, the facility manager at Friar Lake. He had a golden retriever too, though his was white, barely out of puppyhood, and a real handful. He often brought Brody with him to Friar Lake, hoping that Rochester would keep him in line, but the opposite was true. My big goofy golden usually followed his white partner in crime into mischief. However, I was very comfortable leaving Rochester with Joey when I had to head down to campus.

"What are you working on these days?" Joey asked as he scratched Rochester behind the ears. "Anything interesting?"

I told him about the immigration program. "My grandfather came here after World War II," he said. "He got a lot of blowback from other Italians who were worried that he'd been a Fascist, that he'd fought for Mussolini, all that stuff."

"And was he? Did he?"

"Not that he'd ever tell me. He was just a kid then, anyway. It really killed him that it was other Italians that harassed him. He said he expected it from Americans—when he got here he could speak only a few words of English, he had a heavy accent, all he knew how to do was farm work. He expected his *connazionali*, his people, to accept him."

I thought about what Joey had said as I drove down the hill from Friar Lake. Why would other Italians have shunned Joey's grandfather? Was it a case of "close the door behind you?" Were they worried that newcomers would damage the foothold they'd established in the US?

The Eastern campus sprawled over a few dozen acres of hilltop in Leighville, a small town on a crest overlooking the Delaware River. When I'd first seen it as an incoming freshman, I'd been intimidated by the hundred-year-old stone buildings, the broad lawns where students played Frisbee or practiced with nunchucks. How could I ever fit in there?

It had to be what Joey's grandfather, and other immigrants including those in my own family, had faced when they showed up on American shores. I had to learn a new language in order to fit in. Terms like empirical, post-modern and context. Sometimes when my professors spoke I'd lose the thread of meaning when I couldn't immediately define hegemony or dichotomy.

Since then I'd mastered the language enough to become a professor myself. Now those stone buildings were warm and welcoming, holding memories of intellectually challenging seminars and undergraduate antics. It was an interesting metaphor for the immigrant experience and I made a note to include it in planning for the seminar.

I found Professor Del Presto's office in the building where I'd taken my sociology and political science classes years before. She was younger than I'd expected, with long brown hair in a center part over a heart-shaped face. I introduced myself and told her what I'd already come up with in terms of programming.

She said she was eager to help me, because as a grad student she'd done some work with the continuing education department, and enjoyed the different viewpoints adult learners brought.

"One of my academic interests is in social media, and I've been compiling data from Twitter and Facebook posts about immigration and using it to make comparisons with earlier attitudes. Looking at hashtags like #immigration, #uslatino and #noamnesty tell me what people on social media are thinking."

I remembered what Joey had told me about his grandfather's experience. "How do you compare that to what people were saying in the past, before there was Twitter and Facebook?"

"People have been socializing and sharing information and ideas since man developed spoken language," she said. "For my purposes I've been looking at trends in the mass media, particularly when I can find those 'man-in-the-street' reports and interviews. Colonial broadsides, yellow journalism and early iterations of scandal sheets all have given me insight into how people felt at different times about immigrants."

"I've just been rereading Emma Lazarus's sonnet, 'The New

Colossus,' for the Jewish American Lit course I'm teaching," I said. "It's probably one of the most quotable works within that canon, and I remember reading it in elementary school when we studied immigration."

"That's an interesting piece, because it represents an ideal of immigration – Lady Liberty welcoming the huddled masses – that was unrealized then, and even now. Going back as far as the American Revolution, we experienced prejudices against new immigrants from England and Scotland. Americans couldn't believe we'd embrace newcomers from the country we had just battled to leave behind. And then, during the time of the two world wars, people were very suspicious of German, and then Japanese, immigrants."

"And Italian," I said. I told her about Joey's grandfather's experience.

"One of the less appealing attributes of the American experience is the desire to shut the door on anyone coming in behind you."

"And you're finding that expressed today in social media?" "What we think of as a fairly new phenomenon has its roots in

the early computer networks of the 1970s," she said. "As soon as the use of networked computers moved from purely military and government uses, people began using them to share information and ideas. Bulletin board systems, CompuServe, and AOL began to gain traction in the 1980s."

"I was there," I said. "I got my first computer, a Commodore 64, when I was sixteen, and I played around with bigger systems when I was an undergraduate here at Eastern in the late 1980s."

"Then you know how much easier it is to say things when you're shielded by the anonymity of an avatar or a screen name."

I knew from experience the hubris that came from the assumption that what you were doing online couldn't be tracked back to you. It was, after all, the reason I'd been bold enough to hack into Mary's credit reports—I'd thought no one could track the actions back to me.

Wrong.

We talked for a few more minutes about how Professor Del

Presto could shape a program, what kinds of materials she could provide and so on. Once again I was reminded of the excitement of learning something new, of living the life of the mind in an academic environment.

As I drove back to campus, I was at a four-way stop sign behind a pickup truck on high wheels with decal on the back window with some writing squeezed into the shape of North America. I leaned forward and read "Fuck off we are full."

Wow. That was the same sentiment that had sent Lily's parents to Havana and prevented so many other Jews from immigrating to the US. What would Emma Lazarus make of our contemporary attitude toward that "wretched refuse?" Would she still idolize Lady Liberty, lifting her lamp beside the golden door? Would she tell the Old World to keep the huddled masses unless they had the skills necessary for an H-1 B visa or a half million dollars to pour into our tired economy?

Chapter 4
Ethnic Enclaves

The course I'd mentioned to Professor Del Presto that I was teaching was one on Jewish-American Literature. In addition to my administrative work, I often picked up a class in the English department as a way to keep my finger on the pulse of the college, and so I could continue to experience those moments of transitory academic delight like the one I'd shared in the sociology professor's office.

In the past I'd taught freshman comp, technical writing and mystery fiction. Lucas Roosevelt, the chair of the English department, had been very good to me when I returned to Bucks County from prison, giving me my first paid job as an adjunct, so I owed him a bunch of favors. He had called me in the late spring to ask me if I could teach the Jewish-American literature course that fall. It hadn't been offered in a while because there was no one on the full-time faculty interested in teaching it, and he was worried that it would fall out of the catalogue if too much time passed.

I'd taken the course myself as an Eastern undergraduate, so I agreed. I'd been worrying that all the reading and preparation for discussion would be difficult to carry out while running Friar Lake as my full-time job, but so far I'd been enjoying it. That night, as Lili and I relaxed on the couch after dinner, I reviewed my notes on the materials I'd given the students to read in advance of our second meeting the next day.

I'd pulled a couple of excerpts from Abraham Cahan's *The Rise of David Levinsky*, a Horatio Alger rags-to-riches story that epitomized the desire of immigrants to succeed in the New World. I was surprised to note that I'd selected a section in which David distinguishes himself as a scholar of the Talmud while still in Russia, and how that mental rigor presaged his success in business later in life.

"Do you think I should join Rabbi Goldberg's Talmud study group?" I asked Lili. I explained what I'd read in the Cahan excerpt.

"Do you need more mental rigor in your life?" she asked. "Or will studying Talmud make you more successful, like David Levinsky?"

"I think seeing so much death around me and Rochester has made me more conscious of my spiritual side," I said. "And you living with you has reminded me of how much we both remember of those Bible stories we'd learned as kids."

"If you're interested, then follow up. It's not like a gym membership—you won't be locked in for a year."

I said I'd consider it and went back to my reading. Given my concerns with what Joel Goldberg had been worried about, I was surprised that so much of the material I'd selected for the course was connected to what he'd been worrying about. But then, so much of the early works of Jewish American literature had been about those very issues.

The other section I'd chosen from the Cahan novel was about Levinsky's ability to exploit his workers and steal from his competition. I wanted the students to see the darker side of the immigrant experience as well—the way that a former Talmudic scholar could go against his principles in a desperate desire to succeed, even if it left him with "a brooding sense of emptiness and insignificance."

That connected to the prejudice that Joey's grandfather had experienced, that I was sure many immigrants confronted. Sometimes their countrymen were the first to exploit their naiveté and desperation.

All four of my grandparents had come to the United States from Russia soon after the turn of the century. My mother's family had landed in Trenton, and they'd lived in a small neighborhood called Jewtown near the river, a warren of narrow streets and alleys and buildings jammed together. Yiddish was the *lingua franca*, and it wasn't until urban renewal in the sixties destroyed the area that the Jews had been forced to move out and integrate with the rest of the city.

My grandparents had been moderately successful. My mother's father had his own business delivering baked goods to stores and restaurants, and my father had grown up on a family farm in Connecticut, where they had taken in summer boarders who wanted to escape the city heat.

Had they been forced to make the kind of difficult decisions David Levinsky had in order to achieve that success? I was sure of that. They had struggled to put their children through college and establish them in professional careers. They had kept up their religious traditions, from Passover Seders to bar mitzvahs where their sons proclaimed their connection to the generations that had come before them.

Eventually I went back to the course materials, and spent some time reviewing Leo Rosten's *The Education of H*Y*M*A*N K*A*P*L*A*N*, which I'd read as a teenager and still loved. By the time of my class on Tuesday afternoon, I was even more immersed in questions of immigration. I was eager to hear what contemporary students thought about the adult English class Rosten described, and wondered if any of them knew friends or family members who'd taken what we were now calling English as a Second Language, or at the college level, English for Academic Purposes.

We met in a small seminar room on the third floor of Blair Hall, which housed the English and Humanities departments. Tall, gothic-arched windows along one side let in the light and gave students the chance to look outside in case I bored them. Fluorescent lights hung on pendants around the room, and a rich wooden wainscoting ran around the perimeter of the room, a legacy of Eastern's long history of deep-pocket alumni.

I had a dozen students, a mix of men and women. From their names, I guessed that most had some Jewish heritage, but I didn't want to make a big deal of that. Literature was literature, after all. You didn't have to be a woman to read Jane Austen, African-American to appreciate Toni Morrison. All of them were English majors looking for an additional credit toward their requirement, and that was fine with me. I was no scholar of the field and didn't want the students to know more than I did.

They filed in to the classroom in twos and threes, chattering and laughing as they settled into their wooden chairs, assembled seminar-style in a semi-circle around me.

"Let's talk about immigration," I said, once I had taken roll. "Since science has established that humanity originated in Africa, we're all immigrants to this continent, and to what eventually became this country. So the immigrant experience—leaving behind home, family, even language is a common one in American literature. What did you find in reading the excerpts I gave you? Any commonality? Differences?"

A young woman raised her hand. "I was interested in the idea of the ghetto. How in Russia and Poland and places like that Jews were forced to live in specific communities, and then when they came to the United States they did that voluntarily."

Her name was Jessica Sharpstein, and if you'd put her in an apron, with a kerchief on her head, she could have been an extra in a production of *Fiddler on the Roof*.

I nodded. "My grandparents were drawn to places where they had landsmen – people from the same home town. My mother's family ended up in Trenton that way."

"Mine, too," a boy said. His name was Noah Plotnick, a Jewish name if there ever was one. "But the places where they lived were all torn down before I was born."

We talked about ethnic enclaves for a while, how people probably felt safer in them. "No one would criticize you for speaking with an accent," a young woman named Rosita said. "Sometimes in Philadelphia when I'm out with my mother, who's from the Dominican Republic, people complain that it's hard to understand her."

A young black man with a single dreadlock hanging down his back said, "Or walk across the street to avoid you."

A heavyset blonde in a man's button-down shirt over slacks said, "Or yell things at you and tell you to go back where you come from." She had a strong Eastern European accent, and in our introductions the previous week she said she was from Poland.

"I hope that Eastern is that kind of enclave for all of you," I said. "That you all feel safe from discrimination here because of how you look, how you speak, or where your family comes from."

There was a general murmur of agreement. "I was surprised by the mix of ethnic groups in the adult education class in Rosten's book," Rosita said. "That these groups would mingle so much. Where I live in North Philly, the groups are still very separate."

I nodded. "There are still ethnic enclaves, aren't there? Any big city will have a Little India, a Chinatown, a Little Havana. And yet it's hard to stay in one of those areas for most people, isn't it? Rosita, you mentioned people complaining about your mother's accent. Outside your neighborhood?"

She nodded. "I feel like maybe if people mixed more they would get along better."

"This kind of discrimination isn't new." I told them about Professor Del Presto's work looking at the history of prejudice, and its prevalence in social media.

The syllabus moved into more contemporary work, and I asked them to read Philip Roth's novella "Goodbye Columbus" from the collection under the same title before the next class. "Pay particular attention to the themes of assimilation and class distinction," I said. "That's going to be the next step in the immigrant experience."

As I walked back to my car, I thought about Joel Goldberg and his concerns about the Holocaust. Was that kind of obsession symptomatic of schizophrenia? I realized that I knew little about the illness beyond what I'd seen on TV and read in novels. So I detoured past the psychology department, where I was lucky to find Professor Bill Conwell at his office.

I had gotten to know Bill a few months before when he offered a program about combatting dementia at Friar Lake. I'd taken some of his advice myself, like eating foods shown to remove toxins that contributed to Alzheimer's, and I'd gone back to doing the crossword puzzle regularly. And of course, Rochester gave me lots of opportunities for exercise.

"Hey, Steve," he said, getting up from his desk to shake my hand. He was about my age, mid-forties, and very fit – he ran marathons and triathlons in his spare time. "How's it going?"

"Pretty good. I can do the New York Times puzzle every day—though I need a little help on Friday and Saturday."

"That's excellent." He sat back down and I took the chair across from him. "What can I do for you today?"

I told him about my encounter with Joel Goldberg, though I didn't tell him about Joel's death. "It made me curious to know more about schizophrenia."

"You should know about it, because it often shows up in college age students," he said. He sat back in his chair, his hands behind his head. "It's a chronic and severe mental disorder that affects how a person thinks feels and behaves. Those who suffer from it might seem like they've lost touch with reality."

I thought about Joel's behavior at the synagogue the day of the blessing of the animals. "Can they be dangerous?"

He shook his head. "That's one of the common misperceptions. Most schizophrenics aren't violent and don't exhibit aggressive behaviors. Only about a small percentage, ten to fifteen percent."

"What about if someone with schizophrenia feels threatened?"

"In that regard, they're probably like all of us," he said. "The fight or flight response kicks in. What's this about? Has this guy been threatening you, or someone else?"

"Not as far as I know. It was just his behavior when I saw him, and the way that some other people responded."

"That's a tough one. Even loved ones can get tired of someone who's in the throes of a mental illness. And we're always frightened of what we don't know."

We talked for a while longer, and then a student came by to see him so I walked out. Was Joel Goldberg in that small percentage of schizophrenics who were dangerous? Was that why Rabbi Goldberg had been out of touch with his brother, because he was too much to handle?

What if I joined the rabbi's Talmud study group with Rochester, and Joel showed up again, further agitated? Would I be putting myself and my dog in danger?

Chapter 5
Family Connections

When I got home that evening, Lili was on the phone once more, again speaking rapid Spanish, but this time I figured out she was speaking with her brother, Federico.

I fed Rochester and we went out for our evening constitutional. As we walked, I thought about my parents, and how sorry I was that they had never been able to meet Lili. They didn't care for my ex-wife, Mary. But my mother had kept her mouth shut—I'd brought home a Jewish girl, after all, one who was smart and pretty, and that was a lot better than many of the sons of her friends and cousins, and she wasn't one to tempt fate by complaining.

My father, on the other hand, had made it clear in small ways that he thought Mary was too bossy, too sharp-tongued. "You need a wife who will treat you like an equal," he had said to me several times. "That woman talks to you like you work for her."

"It's a relationship, Dad," I'd said. "Modern women have to work twice as hard to succeed as men, and sometimes Mary has a hard time leaving that attitude behind at work."

He had snorted. By the time Mary and I divorced, he was already suffering from the cancer that would kill him, and I was locked up in

California. Our brief phone calls centered mostly around his health, though I could tell he was happy that Mary had moved on.

My father had always appreciated a good-looking woman, and with her curvaceous figure, mass of curly hair and heart-shaped face, Lili radiated beauty. She also had a kindness that Mary lacked, that I was sure he'd have responded well to.

Which led me to considering how I'd get along with Senora Weinstock, when we met in person. She seemed to have a lot of Lili's fire and determination, though underlaid with a sense that the world was against her—conspiring to chase her from her childhood home and leave her to roam the earth unmoored. What would she think of me, a man with a checkered past, too old to give her more grandchildren, not wealthy enough to give her daughter the life she deserved?

When I got home, Lili was still talking, though she'd slipped into English. "I have to go, Fedi. There's only so much I can do in a weekend."

She ended the call with *besos* and *abrazos* for her niece and nephew. Then she turned to me. "*Dios mio!* I told Fedi that I'll come down for a visit, and he jumped all over it. I feel terrible that the burden of all this stuff with my mother is falling on him and Sara."

"They want the burden, don't they?" I asked. "You told me Fedi built a mother-in-law unit onto his house for her. That they want her to move in with them."

"I know. But I feel like it's right for me to go down there. And I admit, maybe, that I'm feeling a little wanderlust. This is the longest I've lived in one place, with one job, in ages."

I was disturbed. "But I thought you wanted to settle down, after all that roving."

"I thought so, too. I still think so. I don't know. I'm just confused."

"Well, you've been at Eastern for two years," I said. "That seems to be your limit, doesn't it?"

She cocked her head and stared at me. "What do you mean?"
"You were married to Philip for what, two years? And Adriano

about the same? Maybe you've got an internal clock that makes you start to get restless after that much time has passed."

"Are you insinuating that I'll leave you, too? Because the situation with both of my ex-husbands was very different."

I held up my hands in surrender. "Hey, I wasn't implying anything. Just stating a point."

"A not very pleasant point." Rochester kept dancing around between us, looking up at us and yipping, and it was difficult to concentrate on what Lili was saying with the dog getting in the way. "Why don't you take your dog and go for a walk?" Lili said.

"We just did that."

"Then call your friend Rick and go over there. I need some time to think without your dog barking and you making smart comments."

I chose not to take any of that personally. Lili was upset, and leaving and taking Rochester with me would give her a chance to calm down.

"Sounds like a good idea to me," I said. I hooked up Rochester's leash once again, and he was confused. Another walk so soon? But he wasn't one to complain.

I'd first met Rick Stemper when we were in a high school chemistry class. We weren't great friends back then, but once I'd returned to Bucks County we had met up by chance and bonded over our divorces. He was a detective with the Stewart's Crossing police department, and soon after Rochester had come into my life, Rick had adopted an Australian Shepherd. Our dogs were as close to each other as Rick and I were.

Outside, I called Rick and asked if I could come over with Rochester and a pizza, and he was all over that idea. I called in a delivery order to Giovanni's, in the shopping center in downtown Stewart's Crossing. Luckily, we both liked the same kind—a thick crust with spicy Italian sausage crumbled and scattered over a base of homemade tomato sauce, freshly sautéed mushrooms and shredded mozzarella from an artisan cheese maker in New Hope.

Rascal was in Rick's backyard, where Rick had installed an agility course to keep his dog busy. I opened the gate, and Rochester rushed inside. The dogs greeted each other at Rick's front door like long-lost brothers, jumping around and trying to hump each other.

Rascal was about six months younger than Rochester but they were both the same size. The Aussie had a white chest and forelegs and a black head, back and rear legs. His muzzle was white with brown cheeks and his nose was as black as trouble—which was what he and Rochester got up to whenever they were together.

I walked up to the front door and rang the bell, and Rick answered a moment later. Though we were the same age, he was graying faster than I was – probably all the stress of police work. He was a couple of inches shorter than I was, and more muscular—I knew that he ran regularly and worked out at the gym a couple of times a week.

"What's up?" he asked, as I walked in.

"Lili's mother is on a rampage." I explained the situation as he handed me a Dogfish Head Firefly Ale, from a Delaware microbrewery we both liked.

His kitchen hadn't been changed much since the house was built in the fifties; he'd put in a new fridge, oven and dishwasher, but the Formica cabinets were original, as was the big stainless steel sink and the brown and tan patterned linoleum floor. It was a comfortable room and I liked hanging out there.

"Lili thought it was a good idea for me to get out of the house for a while, and I agreed."

We watched the dogs romp around the yard for a couple of minutes, chasing and nipping at each other, until Rochester scrambled up the arm of the teeter-totter. He got to the center, caught his balance and woofed once before the other arm lowered down. Then he raced down and began to chase Rascal again.

His least favorite was the set of weave poles – he couldn't seem to get the point of racing to and fro like a crazy dog.

Maybe that's because he was already kind of crazy.

When the pizza arrived, the dogs rushed inside through the doggie door, and while I distracted them with some squeaky toys Rick put two bowls of food out on his kitchen floor. They both chewed noisily, and Rick and I dug in, There was no matching real, Jersey-style pizza from your neighborhood joint, where the mushrooms came from the farmer's market and the sausage and cheese from local farms.

"You should have seen Tiffany's mom when she was on a roll," Rick said. Tiffany was his ex-wife, a Puerto Rican wild child who still depended on Rick now and then. "She'd start talking Spanish a mile a minute and I could never tell if she was excited or pissed off."

"Lili has a brother down in Florida who's been looking after their mom," I said. "She's lucky. So I am I, I guess. Otherwise we might have to have her move in with us."

When there was no more pizza crust for them to snarf down, the dogs went back outside, raced around for a few minutes, and then sprawled together under an oak tree that had turned gold. Rick and I joined them in the autumn evening, sitting on a picnic bench.

"So I have some news," Rick said. "I'm going to ask Tamsen to marry me."

"Wow! That's great. Congratulations." We fist-bumped and both laughed.

Tamsen Morgan was the woman Rick had been dating for almost a year by then. She had lost her husband to the Iraq war a few years before, leaving her with a young son whom Rick coached in Pop Warner football. She had a big family in Stewart's Crossing — parents, sister, cousins—and Rick spent all the holidays with them.

"Have your folks met Tamsen yet?" They had moved to Florida a few years before I returned home.

"Yeah. Remember when my cousin got married in Virginia and Rascal came to stay with you? Tamsen went with me."

"They all got along?"

"What do you think? Tam's beautiful and accomplished and she comes with a ready-made grandson. They were in love." He sat back. "You think I can borrow Lili one Saturday? I need a woman's advice on a ring for Tamsen. I can't ask her sister for help because Tam would kill me if she found out Hannah knew before she did."

I clinked my bottle against Rick's. "I'm sure she'd be delighted. You're making a good move, pal."

"I'm not always sure of that myself, what with my history with Tiffany. But Tam's different, and I feel like a different guy when I'm with her. Better."

"That's the way I feel about Lili. She makes me want to be the guy she deserves. Even if she gets cranky sometimes."

Rick lifted his bottle. "To both of us being better men."

"I'll toast to that." Our bottles clinked once more, and this time the dogs jumped up and rushed over to us, eager to get into the celebration. They were part of our family, too, after all. I was glad that Rick and Rascal had been able to merge so easily with Tamsen and her family—would Rochester and I be able to do the same thing with Lili's?

When I got home, Lili was on the phone with another relative, and I had to wait until she was finished to tell her about Rick's plan to propose to Tamsen, and his request that she help him pick out a ring. Lili was delighted to help, and immediately called Rick. I listened to her side of the conversation, how she thought Tam would like a diamond set off with her birthstone emerald because it matched her green eyes.

I was fascinated by how happy Lili seemed with all the marriage and ring stuff, and I wondered if she was being completely honest with me about not wanting to get married again. She'd been through it twice—a city hall visit with her first husband, a ceremony at a palazzo in Venice with her second—and since both marriages had ended in divorce she'd always said she wasn't eager to replicate the situation.

But hearing her talk, I wondered if she was secretly harboring a desire for a proposal from me. I'd only been married once, in a big traditional Jewish ceremony complete with a huppah, monogrammed yarmulkes and the broken glass. I'd never formally asked Mary to marry me—we'd mutually decided that if we were going to move to California together so that she could accept a big promotion, it made sense for us to marry so that I'd get health coverage through her, at least until I found a job myself.

Not the most romantic of situations, but then, our marriage had been like that—doing the things we thought we should, like buying a house and trying to have children. When I went to prison and she divorced me, I was sad and felt like a failure, but my heart wasn't broken.

If something happened to Lili, or we split up, though, I had a feeling the emotional fallout would be much worse. I had much stronger feelings for her than I ever did for Mary. We punctuated our conversations with "love you" all the time. When I saw sappy movies I felt a twinge in my heart that made me connect with those emotions on screen. Flipping through channels one day we'd landed on *Grease*, and when Danny and Sandy sang "You're the one that I want" I felt my eyes well up as I reached for Lili's hand.

Despite that, I believed that a marriage license was just a piece of paper, one that often caused more complications than the joy it brought. Earlier that night, Lili had said she was feeling some wanderlust, and yet here she sounded so enthusiastic about marriage. Was putting a ring on her finger the way to keep her beside me?

Women. Who could understand them? Good thing Rochester was a boy dog or I'd be completely lost.

Chapter 6
Fog

A cold front moved in that night, and Wednesday morning when I took Rochester for his walk around River Bend, fog lingered on the manicured lawns and the piles of fallen leaves. I fed Rochester, hurried through my own breakfast and skipped the crossword puzzle so that we could get to the Talmud study group on time.

Lili was still asleep by the time my dog and I were ready to leave, but I lingered a moment in the doorway of the bedroom. She always scrubbed off whatever makeup she'd worn as part of her bedtime ritual, and in the clear light coming in through the window I could see every laugh line, every crow's foot, a few strands of silver in her auburn hair. Those little imperfections made me love her even more, and as I blew her a goodbye kiss, I vowed I'd do whatever I had to in order to keep her by my side.

Since there was little to see through the fog, Rochester slumped into the front seat beside me as we drove through what had been farmland when I was a kid but was now a welter of suburban developments. He perked up as I pulled into a parking space in the lot at Shomrei Torah, perhaps remembering the blessing of a few days before and hoping for another.

Or thinking of Sadie, the female golden.

The rabbi's hybrid sedan was parked in his reserved spot, along with a half-dozen other cars in the lot. Aaron Feinberg, the synagogue president, pulled up and parked as Rochester was nosing a row of azalea bushes. "Your dog is a Talmud scholar, too?" he asked. He held out his hand for Rochester to sniff, but the big golden was too intent on pulling toward some other scent.

"He likes to get his nose into everything." At that moment the golden's big black nose was down to the ground, intent on something ahead of us.

Feinberg wore a dark blue pinstripe suit with a white shirt and a red power tie, and I worried that I looked like a *schlep* in my polo shirt and khakis. Saul Benesch and Henry Namias arrived together, and Feinberg waited in the parking lot for them as Rochester tugged me forward.

He wanted to go in the wrong direction, though, toward the sanctuary, and I had to keep a tight hold on his leash and nearly drag him around the corner to the entrance to the rabbi's study.

There were three other men and two women sitting in a semicircle of chairs in the room when we walked in, all of them in their forties or fifties. Rabbi Goldberg sat in his ergonomic desk chair facing them. His desk was in one corner, crowded with papers and framed photos of him and Sadie. On the edge of the desk was a bright green piece of malachite, with a depression in the center that made me recognize it as a worry stone, the kind you rubbed with your thumb whenever you were stressed. I should probably get one of those. It would come in handy when Rochester was getting into trouble.

I sat beside one of the women and let Rochester off his leash. He immediately hustled over to Sadie to give her a good morning sniff. While I waited for the session to begin, I looked around at the walls lined with bookshelves, most of them half-empty, the gaps between books filled with menorahs, a statue of a fiddler on a roof, and other bits of Judaica.

When Feinberg, Namias and Benesch arrived and took the last three seats, the rabbi introduced me to the group, and everyone seemed very welcoming. I was curious to know how such a study session would operate – had there been homework I didn't know about? Would we be reading in English or Hebrew – which I could only sound out if the vowels were present?

"This is an interesting time in the annual cycle of reading the Torah," the rabbi began. "We're wrapping up the past year and preparing for the new one. Since a year encompasses a great deal of events, so do our services in the month of Elul. As we prepare for the redemption offered us by Yom Kippur, we focus on what I like to call the three T's: Torah, *tefilah*, and *tzedakah*."

He smiled. "Unfortunately saying Torah, prayer, and deeds of kindness doesn't give that satisfying sense of alliteration."

Now the rabbi was speaking my language – peppering English-major terms like alliteration into his speech, and it didn't look like there would be any reading. I relaxed.

It had been a tumultuous year since last Rosh Hashanah, I thought. Rochester and I had been involved in several murder investigations, and we'd put ourselves in danger more than I was comfortable with. I hoped that the new year would be one of peace.

Then the rabbi continued. "The blessings for this service are found in this week's Torah portion, *Parshas Ki Seitzei*. This deals with a Jew's 'going out to war,' i.e., going out to involvement within our material world."

Uh-oh. That didn't sound good. Rochester and I had seen enough of our own kind of war.

We began to talk in Socratic fashion, as Rabbi asked us how we thought we could spread *tzedakah*, or blessings, in the material world, to prepare our souls for our reckoning with God during the Days of Awe between Rosh Hashanah and Yom Kippur.

Rochester eventually settled down between me and an older man named Daniel Epstein, whose name I knew because he was often listed in the program for Sabbath services as the greeter, who handed out prayerbooks and welcomed everyone to shul.

In response to the rabbi's question about *tzedakah*, Epstein said that in the past he'd made his charitable contributions at the end of the calendar year, for tax purposes. "But I've begun to spread them out during the year," he said. "I know a lot of charities rely on contributions to function, and it's hard to budget if all your donations come in during a few weeks in December."

"That's an interesting approach," Rabbi Goldberg said. "And it provides you the blessing of tzedakah throughout the year, instead of just in a short period."

"When I was in Sunday school here, my parents gave me a dime every week for *keren ami*," I said. "Do kids still do that?"

The rabbi laughed. "Yes, we still collect charitable contributions for the State of Israel from Sunday school students, though they usually bring a dollar now. You're right, it's an excellent way to get them into the habit of making regular charitable contributions, though most often that money comes from their parents rather than their own pockets." He sat back in his chair. "And you, Steve? How do you prepare?"

"Well, I work for Eastern College," I said. "So I'm still in that academic routine of believing that the year starts in September, like on the Jewish calendar. My regular job involves computer work and administration, but I occasionally teach a course as an adjunct instructor. This fall I'm teaching one on Jewish American Literature, so I've been reading a lot about the immigrant experience and thinking about my own family history, in the old country, in Trenton, and here at Shomrei Torah."

We continued around the room. Feinberg spoke about how his father survived the Holocaust and what that meant to him. I noticed that Henry Namias glared at him as he spoke, and I wondered why. Was it bragging to say you had a survivor in your family? Why would Namias be bothered?

My reverie was interrupted by a knock on the door, followed by a middle-aged black man stepping inside. "I'm sorry to interrupt, rabbi, but there's a problem." He was out of breath, as if he'd been running, and his hands were shaking.

The man was dressed like I was, in khaki slacks and a polo shirt, but his was embossed *Temple Shomrei Torah,* and he wore a name tag that identified him as Walter Johnson, Facility Manager.

"What is it, Walter?" the rabbi asked.

"I had to call the police. There's a man's body behind the sanctuary. I found him when I was walking around the property."

"What do you mean, a body?" Feinberg demanded. "He's dead, Mr. Feinberg."

The group erupted in murmurs to each other as Johnson moved over to the rabbi to speak more closely to him. Johnson had left the door to the study open, and as he passed me, Rochester jumped up and took off out the door.

"Rochester!" I scrambled out of my seat. "Sorry, sorry," I said as I moved past Johnson and hurried out the door, leaving behind a hubbub. I followed Rochester's erect, plumy tail as he rushed along the side of the sanctuary building. Then he disappeared around the corner.

That was the direction where he'd been trying to go as we walked in. Had he scented the body and tried to tell me about it? Dumb human that I was, I had only about five million scent glands in my nose, whereas a large breed like the golden retriever had nearly three hundred million. So I hadn't sniffed out the problem the way he had, and instead of following his instincts, I'd dragged him into the rabbi's study.

I heard a siren in the distance as I rounded the corner. Tendrils of fog still hung in the air, but I saw Rochester sitting at his alert position beside a man's body, on the ground beside the back wall. The man's face was turned away from me, but as I observed him I got a sinking feeling. He wore a gray T-shirt torn at the neck, then a plaid shirt, with a pea coat over that. His jeans were ragged at the cuffs, and he wore stained white tennis shoes. His brown hair was shaggy and his beard was unkempt. There was a dark stain on the grass beside him that I thought was probably blood.

When I moved around so that I could see his face, I realized my instinct had been correct. It was Joel Goldberg. The rabbi's brother.

Chapter 7
Bad Times

Rochester looked up at me woefully from his position beside Joel Goldberg's body. How long had the man been dead? Could we have saved him if I'd listened to my dog's instincts? From the way the dark fluid had congealed on the ground, and the stiffness in Joel's limbs from the onset of rigor mortis, even if we'd gotten there a half hour earlier, we couldn't have done anything to save him.

The rabbi arrived behind us a moment later, Sadie by his side. "My God! Joel!" A dozen feet behind him the rest of the Talmud study group rushed toward us.

Rochester arose from his position on the ground and moved over to join Sadie by the rabbi's side. Rabbi Goldberg began to kneel, but I took his arm. "In case this is a crime scene, Rabbi, better not to compromise it."

"A crime scene? But why would someone kill my brother?"

"I don't know," I said gently. I pointed at the pool of congealed blood around Joel's head. "But it looks to me like someone did."

The rabbi looked down at his brother. "What were you doing here, Joel?" he asked. "What did you want from me?"

I looked at the rabbi. His face was a rictus of grief, his lips turned down, his eyes watering. His back was slightly hunched, as if he'd lost the will to stand upright.

I had a different question. When did Joel arrive at the temple? Buses did not run all night, so assuming he was still reliant on public transportation, he had to have gotten there the night before.

"When was the last time you saw your brother?" I asked. "Sunday. He ran off before I could talk to him."

A police cruiser arrived, lights flashing and a siren going.

The rabbi's mouth dropped open, and he said, "My parents," in a broken voice, as a uniformed officer got out of the car. "I'll have to call them."

He looked around as if he was searching for his phone, and I put my hand on his shoulder. "That can wait a few minutes," I said. "They're in Arizona, aren't they?"

He nodded.

"Then it's a couple of hours earlier. Let them have their sleep."

The officer came up to us, a stocky young guy in a black uniform, his belt laden with the apparatus of criminal justice. The rabbi, the two dogs and I stepped back to allow him officer to examine Joel's body, and it was clear from his face that Joel was dead. As the other members of the Talmud study group came to comfort the rabbi, I pulled out my cell phone and hit the speed dial button for Rick Stemper. As one of only two detectives on the Stewart's Crossing police force, he was likely to be called to this scene.

"Can't talk now," he said. "On my way to a dead body." "At Shomrei Torah. Rochester and I are here."

He groaned. "Not the dog again. He didn't find the body, did he?"

"Not for want of trying." I explained how we'd been walking toward the rabbi's study, and Rochester was eager to head off to where Joel's body had been discovered.

"I'm almost there. Don't go anywhere."

When I hung up I looked over at Rabbi Goldberg, who was crying. Aaron Feinberg had his arm around the rabbi's shoulders, speaking quietly to him. Walter Johnson and the group from Talmud study stood awkwardly aside, no one sure what to do.

The uniformed officer asked everyone to stay a few feet away from the body as he began laying out crime scene tape. Then Rick arrived, his police badge at his hip, right in front of his holstered pistol. He introduced himself and asked that everyone wait for the officer to get all our details, so that he could interview us later.

"Why us?" Saul Benesch asked. "We didn't see anything." "How long will this take?" another man asked.

"I have to get to work," one of the women said, though I was pretty sure the Talmud study group would have still been going on, if not for the interruption.

"We'll get you on your way as soon as possible," Rick said. He glared at me, which I took to mean that I was exempted from that order.

I didn't want the rabbi to have to stand there in the dissipating fog and watch as his brother's body was investigated by the police and the crime scene team. "The deceased is Rabbi Goldberg's brother," I said to Rick. "Why don't Rochester and I take the rabbi into his study and wait for you there."

Feinberg turned to me, in full presidential mode. "You know this detective?"

"I do," I said. "Rick and I went to Pennsbury High together." "He'll do a good job?" Out of the corner of my eye I saw Rick

quirk an eyebrow at Feinberg's question. "The best," I said.

"Good."

The officer said, "If you'll all follow me, please," and he led the group out to the parking lot where his cruiser was parked.

Rochester sniffed at Sadie. By some mutual agreement, the two goldens turned back toward the rabbi's office, and the rabbi and I followed them.

Once in his office, the rabbi collapsed into his chair, with Sadie on one side of him and Rochester on the other. Sadie sat up and nuzzled his hand. I knew how much that kind of contact could help when you were sad. Rochester had comforted me on many occasions in just the same way.

"I'm so sorry about your brother," I said, as I sat in the middle of the semi-circle of folding chairs. "Do you want to talk about him while we wait?"

"Joel is three years older than I am." He grimaced. "Was."

Rochester rested his head on the rabbi's knee, and the rabbi petted him.

"My big brother," the rabbi said after a moment. "I idolized him when I was a kid. He was smart and funny, a champion debater in high school. He was going to be a lawyer, but his freshman year in college he had a breakdown."

He reached for a tissue from a box on his desk, wiped his eyes and blew his nose. "It took two years to get a diagnosis. Paranoid schizophrenia. My parents worried that there was a genetic reason for his illness, but except for one set of grandparents who survived the camps, most of our family was wiped out in the Holocaust and all their records lost."

The rabbi continued after a moment. "Joel was in and out of treatment facilities for years after that. When he took his medication, he was okay. My father was an optometrist, and Joel worked in his office when he could. But after a few months he'd start to feel like he was seeing the world through a fuzzy cloud, and he'd stop taking the pills and have an episode. Sometimes it was as simple as a kind of disorganization, losing track of what he was doing, losing his keys and wallet and anything else he carried. The worst were when he'd become paranoid—hearing voices in the walls, obsessing about the actions of a neighbor or a store clerk."

I had a college friend with a schizophrenic sister, so I knew a little of what he was going through. "That must have been awful for your parents."

"It was." He stopped to blow his nose again. "My father had a heart attack a couple of years ago, and he and my mother retired to Florida, to one of those senior communities where you have to be fifty-five or older. They wouldn't say so, but I know it was so that they'd have a reason not to have Joel come live with them again. My brother could be... difficult, especially when he was off his meds."

"Did he live with you then?"

He shook his head, and I could see the sadness in his expression. "No, I had no idea where he was. The last time I saw him was when I was working in Milwaukee with a small congregation. Joel showed up in the middle of services one Saturday morning, looking pretty much like you saw him on Sunday. He began to yell, something about how the government was trying to lock people up in camps again. I had to leave the bema to take him out of the sanctuary. The cantor took over for me, and the next day Joel disappeared again, but after my year's contract was up the temple chose not to renew it."

I remembered that Saul Benesch had mentioned a problem in Milwaukee. "Just because of your brother?" I asked.

"It wasn't the first time he'd caused problems, but it was the worst. I couldn't promise them that Joel would never show up again."

Of course he couldn't. And what caring congregation would make such a demand?

"I tried to be a good brother," the rabbi said. "When Joel was first diagnosed, I was sixteen, in confirmation class at our temple. I researched Jewish approaches to mental illness as my project. I thought there had to be a way to pray Joel back to health." "Where was Joel then?"

"In and out of rehab. After I graduated from rabbinical school I got a job as an assistant rabbi at a temple in Arizona, and I asked him to come live with me. He hated the heat and he disappeared after a couple of months. Since then, our contact has been sporadic."

"You didn't know he was in this area?"

"Not at all. Now I wonder—was he coming to see me this morning to ask for help? I saw all that blood around his head. Do you think maybe he took some kind of drug, or had a stroke or a heart attack or something, or then fell and hit his head?"

I didn't want to get into the technical details of rigor mortis, but I said, "I don't think he came here this morning. More likely he arrived last night. What time does the synagogue close?"

He sniffed, and thought for a moment. "The office closes at five, but sometimes we have evening events, or rent out the auditorium to outside groups. Let me check the schedule."

He wheeled his chair back to his desk and typed at his computer for a moment. "The cantor was here until seven with bar mitzvah students. She would have locked up the building when she left."

He began to cry quietly. "If I'd been here, maybe I could have helped him. Called an ambulance, taken him to an emergency room. Instead, he died. By himself."

Both dogs sat up and nuzzled him. He petted them as the tears streamed down his face.

What if Joel hadn't been alone when he died? There was no rock or other hard object near his body, and the blood around his head indicated to me that he had died where he lay. Could someone have killed him? And if so, who?

I waited until the rabbi had regained his composure to ask, "What was it Joel was so eager to show you on Sunday?"

"I don't know. By the time I got back to my office after blessing all the animals, Joel was gone. But I did notice that he'd been using my computer."

"How could you tell?"

"There were dozens of browser windows open, including the list of our board of directors, and at least two or three windows for each member. That was typical Joel. He never closed a browser window because he was always worried he'd need to go back."

"Did you tell the board that Joel had been researching them? That they ought to be wary of him, let you know if he approached them?"

He shook his head. "You don't know what it's like to deal with a schizophrenic. Sometimes he gets – got – these ideas in his head and wouldn't let go, but other times he'd completely forget what he was doing and move on to something else." He took a deep breath. "I didn't think there was really anything to worry about."

There was a knock on the door, and when it opened Rick looked in. "Good morning, Rabbi. I'm sorry to trouble you now, but I need to ask you a few questions about your brother."

"Was he – murdered?" Rabbi Goldberg asked.

"I can't make a judgment right now, I'm afraid. I need to look at the evidence and investigate the situation. There appears to be some evidence of blunt force trauma to his head, and the coroner will have to perform an autopsy, as well as toxicology tests."

"How long will it be before we can bury him?" Rabbi Goldberg asked. "It's our tradition that we bury our dead as soon as possible."

"I'm sorry, but I can't say. The Coroner's office will be in touch with you when they can release your brother's body."

"My parents will need time to make arrangements," he said. "Can you ask them to let me know as soon as possible?"

Rick agreed, and I said, "Rochester and I will wait outside, in case there's anything else we can do for you, Rabbi."

I hooked up Rochester's leash, and we walked outside. I let him lead the way, and we walked back to where Joel's body rested. The police had placed small plastic markers around the body, and a woman in a Tyvek suit and booties was collecting evidence.

Rochester turned abruptly toward the parking lot and began to stalk there, nose to the ground. "What's up, boy?" I asked, but I let him tug me forward.

We crossed the paved lot, heading toward the street as cars whizzed past. He stopped and began to paw at the ground. "What's there, Rochester?"

He lowered his head to sniff at a beautiful green malachite stone like the one I'd seen on the rabbi's desk, the striations of dark and light providing a beautiful pattern. When I crouched down to get a closer look, I could see that the depression in the center looked well-rubbed.

In the past, Rochester had been very good at finding pieces of evidence that a human investigator might have overlooked, so I approached this situation with caution. Sure, the stone could have belonged to anyone, but it was only a couple of feet from the bus stop, and on Sunday Joel Goldberg had arrived at Shomrei Torah by bus. Add that to the matching stone on the rabbi's desk, and there was a reasonable chance that the worry stone had belonged to Joel.

I pulled a tissue from my pocket and wrapped the stone in it, careful not to smudge and potential fingerprints. I stood, and praised Rochester profusely, rubbing him behind his ears the way he loved.

We began to walk back toward the synagogue. As we approached the door to the rabbi's study, Rick and the rabbi came out, Sadie walking without a leash beside them. "Thank you for help," Rick said. "And again, I'm very sorry for your loss."

The rabbi nodded. I walked over to them and opened the worry stone in my palm. "Do you recognize this?" I asked him.

"That was my brother's stone," he said. He reached for it, but I pulled my hand back and instead handed the stone to Rick, who pulled an evidence bag from his pocket and took the stone from me.

"Our parents went to Greece when we were teenagers and brought back one for each of us," the rabbi said. "Joel still had it the last time I saw him. He said it calmed him down to hold it and rub his thumb over it."

"Where did you find this?" Rick asked.

"Face the bus stop sign and then walk about three paces to the right." I turned to the rabbi and asked, "Do you think it could have fallen from Joel's pocket when he got off the bus?"

"Joel wouldn't have been that careless," he said. "He'd have been holding it in his hand, especially if he'd just been on a bus. Traveling always made him nervous."

"Could someone have taken it from him?" Rick asked. "I don't see why."

As Rochester and Sadie sniffed each other, I turned to the rabbi. "Why don't I walk you back to your study, Rabbi. Is there someone you can call? You shouldn't be alone at a time like this. The cantor? Another rabbi?"

"I should call the cantor," he said. "She'll want to know."

Rick followed my directions toward the street, and the rabbi and I walked back to his office, accompanied by the two dogs. When we got inside, Rochester and Sadie settled together in a corner and the rabbi picked up the phone. I tried not to eavesdrop, but I did hear that the cantor would be there shortly.

I was about to make my apologies and leave, when the rabbi stood up and began pacing around the office. "I just don't understand," he said. "Joel's behavior was always somewhat opaque when he was suffering through an episode, but usually I could make sense of what he wanted."

He picked up a piece of paper from his desk. "Your detective friend left me something," he said. "He said Joel had an old-fashioned photo postcard folded up in his shoe. He let me take a photo copy of it, but it doesn't make any sense to me. Maybe you'll have a different perspective."

He handed the paper to me. It was in sepia tones, and showed two dark-haired boys under a tree. They wore white shirts and shorts held up by suspenders. On the back "Kalman, 15 *und* Aaron, 10" had been written in a spidery hand.

"You don't recognize either of these boys?" I asked.

"No. And no one in our family has those names. Why would my brother have that picture hidden in his shoe?"

"Do you think this was what he wanted to show you?" "Perhaps. But why? Where did it come from?"

"Could he have found it somewhere? And that's why he came to this area, to find you and give it to you?"

"I don't even know how long he was here before he showed up on Sunday," he said. He looked at me quizzically. "You told Aaron Feinberg that you were a bar mitzvah at the old shul in Trenton. Do you know the area well?"

"I guess," I said. "I was away for a long time."

"Joel showed up on Sunday on the bus from Trenton, and all he was carrying was his backpack. He had to have brought more with him—I know he had a ratty old winter coat he would never have given up, and he usually had a bag of books with him, too. Can you help me find out where he was staying, and find the rest of his personal effects for me? I don't know Trenton at all, and I'd appreciate your help trying to navigate the city and understand where he was and what he was doing."

I felt a familiar tingle and the chance to explore the background of a crime. The rabbi had his congregation to tend to, and I was sure that the loss of his brother would weigh heavily on him. Seeing the places where his brother had been would probably be very upsetting.

There was no question I could deny the rabbi's request. And it would be a harmless way to indulge the curiosity that had gotten me into trouble so often in the past.

"I'd be happy to help, Rabbi," I said. "If he was homeless he might have been staying at one of the shelters in Trenton, and I can go over there for you. Do you have a recent photo of your brother you could email me?"

"The newest one I have is a couple of years old, but it should serve."

I gave him my email address, then roused Rochester from his place by Sadie. "I'm so sorry, Rabbi," I said. "I'm an only child, but I'm sure it must be devastating to lose a sibling."

"I lost Joel years ago," he said sadly. "But now, with your help, maybe I can find a piece of him again."

Chapter 8
Death Dog

As Rochester and I walked to the parking lot, I saw Rick working with a crime scene tech to block off an area near the bus sign with yellow tape. He met us halfway to my car, still wearing blue gloves on his hands.

"How'd you notice the stone?" he asked. "Rochester."

He groaned. "The death dog," he said. "I swear sometimes I think we ought to just put a little uniform on him and let him do all the work."

Rochester had what I called a nose for crime, and he'd found clues several times that had helped Rick solve cases. "He can't use a computer," I said. "His paws are too big for the keyboard. So there'd still be a job for you."

"Ha-ha."

"How come you're out here, anyway?" I asked. "Isn't this outside the Stewart's Crossing town limits?"

"Yeah, this is Central Makefield Township out here, and their department handles DUI, home invasions, drugs in the schools, that kind of thing. They don't have the staff or the skills to handle a possible homicide, so they come to us."

"You think it's murder?"

"Unless he banged himself on the head with some as yet unknown object, dropped it somewhere we haven't looked yet, and then staggered over to the building."

"The rabbi asked me to look into where Joel has been the last few days," I said. "If that doesn't interfere with your investigation, of course."

"Whatever you can find. And I want to talk to you later, get some more background on this rabbi."

I looked at my watch. "I should get to work. But I can meet you at the Drunken Hessian at six. First round's on you."

He grunted an assent, then petted Rochester and told him to get busy solving the case. Rochester licked Rick's hand in response.

My dog and I drove up the River Road, where lush willows drooped over the banks and swamp maples held their vibrant green leaves for a few more weeks. I turned to Rochester, sitting beside me on the front passenger seat. "You found the place where the rabbi's brother was hit. Any other clues?"

He sat with his nose pressed against the window and appeared to be fascinated by cows in a field. So, no help from him.

"Poor Rabbi Goldberg, having to live with a brother with mental illness, and then losing him," I said to Rochester. Incidents like that made me glad that I was an only child, though I'd spent most of my youth wishing for a brother or a sister.

Rochester slumped down into the seat without voicing an opinion.

Dogs. What can you do?

I spent most of the day thinking about the immigration program and how I could incorporate Professor Del Presto's research into an exploration of contemporary attitudes toward the topic. I got sidetracked, as often happens when I plunge into research, and read a lot about the restrictions that had been in place when my grandparents and Lili's had left Eastern Europe, and how many of those restrictions were still in place. Lili's ex-boyfriend, Van Driver, was a reporter for the *Wall Street Journal,* and I read an article he'd written about a Syrian refugee family that had been sponsored for settlement in Canada by a charitable group.

Now that the parents and their two children were safe, however, they were besieged by relatives back in Syria or in refugee camps in Lebanon, asking for help. "It is my brother," the father of the family had said. "How can I refuse him? But while we still depend on charity, what can I do?"

I remembered a conversation with my grandmother once, when she expressed guilt that she had been able to escape before the Holocaust, while her cousins and other family members were sent to camps and murdered. She told me that her father had gone back to Lithuania to visit his younger brother, to convince him and his family to come to the United States, but they wouldn't leave. That he hunted for years after the war to find out what had happened to them, eventually learning how they had died.

As far as I knew, I had no rabbis in my family tree, but back in Lithuania, my great-grandfather had been a *tzadik,* a righteous man who went to morning worship every day, a layman who had devoted himself to study while his wife ran their leather-tanning business. He'd probably have been pleased that at least one of his descendants was coming back into the flock.

Would he still look for answers in the Torah? I came from generations and generations of people of the book, who had looked to those ancient words for guidance on how to live their lives. And here I was, in the twenty-first century, doing the same thing by attending the sessions with Rabbi Goldberg.

Had we learned so little since those dark days of World War II? People were still suffering and dying all around the world. But the solution couldn't be to bring them all here. My head began to ache at the complexity of it all. Perhaps Professor Del Presto could help a group of interested people make sense of it all. That was the point of Friar Lake, after all.

Around four o'clock Lili texted me that she had another

marathon phone call scheduled with her brother that evening, and it might be a good idea if I went out, as she was likely to be in a bad mood when it ended.

I called her and let her know I'd made plans with Rick. "We're meeting at the Drunken Hessian to talk about a body."

"Not another one. Steve, don't you find it disturbing how dead bodies keep dropping in your path? After all, these are real people, with families and friends, and their lives get cut short."

"I know. And I'm starting to feel like this is almost a calling, to help those people have justice. But in this case, Rochester and I didn't have anything to do with this one. We just happened to be at Talmud study when the body was discovered. It was Rabbi Goldberg's brother – you know, the homeless man who showed up at the blessing of the animals on Sunday."

"The poor man," she said, and I wasn't sure if she meant the rabbi or his brother. "Was it natural causes? Oh, wait, nobody around you dies of natural causes."

"Then are you sure you want me to meet your mother?"

"Don't get me started. When you speak to the rabbi next, be sure to send him my condolences."

When I hung up the phone, I looked at Rochester, who had brought a pebble in from our lunchtime walk and was sniffing it. That reminded me of Joel Goldberg and his worry stone. I took the pebble away from Rochester so he wouldn't break a tooth on it, and turned back to my computer.

From the SEPTA website, I checked the bus schedule for the night before. The latest bus Joel could have taken would have gotten him to Shomrei Torah shortly after eleven PM. Of course, it was possible that Joel had gotten there earlier, but according to Rabbi Goldberg the cantor had closed up the building at seven that evening. Unless Joel had arrived while she was tutoring, and hidden on the property, it was likely he'd gotten there after she had already left.

For a moment I considered her as a suspect. But I had seen her when I'd attended services, and she was a petite woman, not tall enough to have cracked Joel Goldberg over the head. She hadn't been at the blessing of the animals, and I had no reason to suspect that she even knew of Joel's existence. Even so, I sent a quick email to Rick with what I'd discovered.

Because Rick had asked about the rabbi, I Googled him and discovered that he was thirty years old and held an MA in Hebrew Letters and Literature from Hebrew Union College, the *yeshiva* for Reform rabbis. He had worked as a hospital chaplain in Seattle for two years after graduating, which tied in with his interest in Jewish healing.

Then he had been hired as assistant rabbi by an inner-city temple in Milwaukee coping with a declining membership. Soon after he left, the congregation had combined with another in the suburbs along Lake Michigan.

I wondered if his departure from the pulpit there had as much to do with demographics as with his brother's outburst, but I couldn't be sure.

The rabbi regularly blogged a version of his sermon, and maintained the temple's website himself. He also tweeted tidbits of Jewish history and culture and posted photos of the temple's *sukkah* and holiday celebrations on Instagram. In addition to the Talmud study group, he hosted a monthly Jewish-themed movie night, and took the youth group on field trips to places of Jewish interest like New York's Lower East Side and The National Museum of American Jewish History in Philadelphia.

Quite impressive for a young rabbi, especially a single one without a wife to help him. But then, maybe his bachelorhood was the reason why he had so much time for the temple. I'd scaled back my outside activities once I had Lili in my life.

Or was his single status a result of his difficult family background? I imagined it would be tough enough to find a woman willing to take on the unpaid job of being a *rebbetzin*, a rabbi's wife, without the additional burden of a mentally ill sibling.

I shut down my computer and stood up. The rabbi's situation

made my problems with Lili and her mother seem small by comparison. But at least I had some information to share with Rick that evening.

Chapter 9
Tough Day

After I took Rochester home, fed and walked him, and kissed Lili goodbye in the midst of her phone call with her brother, I drove into the center of Stewart's Crossing. The Drunken Hessian has been at the corner of Main and Ferry Streets, right by the town's only traffic light, since Revolutionary times. For Rick and me, it was more important as a part of our youth, when the drinking age in Pennsylvania was twenty-one but sometimes you could get a sympathetic bartender at the Hessian to slip you a beer on the sly.

Rick was already in a booth in the back with a pitcher of beer and two glasses. I slid in across from him and poured a beer for myself. "Tough day?"

He nodded. "Any day that begins with a dead body qualifies."

He lifted his glass I touched mine to his in a toast. "To both of us staying alive another day," I said.

He sipped his beer, then put it down. "So what were you doing at the synagogue this morning? I didn't think you were that religious."

I explained about going to Shomrei Torah as a kid and then returning for Yahrzeit prayers, and then the blessing of the animals on Sunday. "The rabbi invited me to join his study group, and when he said I could bring Rochester that clinched it for me."

"What do you know about him?" Rick asked.

I passed on what I had learned about the rabbi's background, as well as Joel's outburst in Milwaukee, and the congregation's refusal to continue his contract. But I added that the temple had closed down soon, so it was hard to be certain.

"Do you think the rabbi had a motive to kill his brother?" Rick asked.

"Is Rabbi Goldberg a suspect?" I asked.

"I'm not eliminating anybody. The rabbi lives alone, and nobody can verify his whereabouts last night. He was pretty shaken up, and that could be grief—or guilt. Maybe he was worried that Joel would screw up this job for him. Sounds like he's been working pretty hard to hold onto it."

"He wouldn't be the first to commit fratricide," I said. "That goes all the way back to Cain and Abel. He seems like a nice guy, and he was definitely broken up by his brother's death." I took another sip of beer. "You know what killed Joel?"

"Preliminary report from the coroner is that he suffered a heavy blow to his head with a blunt object. Not much to go on."

"I assume you didn't find any suspicious blunt objects around the body?"

"Nope. I had the evidence techs comb the area but they didn't come up with much. The guy had a couple of bucks in his pocket and a bus ticket stub, and that's about it."

"And that photograph in his shoe. The rabbi showed me the copy you left with him. You think it's a clue to something?"

"No idea. The guy was schizophrenic, right? So it could mean anything or nothing."

"Time of death?" I asked.

"Sometime late last night. Coroner will get a more precise time to me tomorrow."

"You got my email, right? If we eliminate the cantor as suspect, and assume that she wouldn't have locked up and left the property if

Joel was hanging around, then we can time his arrival at the temple between seven and the time of the last bus, around eleven PM."

The waitress came over and we ordered cheeseburgers and fries. "I spoke to her this morning," he said. "She confirmed what the rabbi said, that she'd locked up at seven. The boy's mom dropped him off at six, and they spent an hour in the sanctuary going over the prayers. When the mom came back at seven, the three of them walked out together. She didn't see anyone around the property, but she admitted that all she did was lock the front door and set the alarm."

He sipped at his beer. "I called the mom, and she confirmed the story. She said she and her son walked out with the cantor, and that theirs were the last cars in the parking lot."

"You had a busy day."

He nodded. "I also interviewed the receptionist and Walter Johnson, the property manager. Johnson didn't know anything about the rabbi having a brother, but the receptionist said she overheard the synagogue president complaining to the rabbi about what happened on Sunday. That was the first she heard of the brother."

"They're the only staff?"

Rick nodded. "You said the rabbi asked you to figure out where his brother had been in Trenton." He poured another round for both of us. "How are you going to that?"

"On Sunday, Joel was pretty agitated, and it sounded like he had some kind of problem he wanted to talk to his brother about. I asked the rabbi, and he said he didn't know. His computer was on when he got back, and from the search history he realized that Joel had spent some time on the computer looking up the names and addresses of members of the congregation's board of directors."

"Interesting." He pulled out his small spiral-bound notebook and wrote something down. "Any idea why?"

"The rabbi thought perhaps he disappeared without saying anything more was because he was upset at the way a couple of the members tried to strong arm him off the property on Sunday. Maybe he wanted to know their names."

The waitress brought our cheeseburgers, and I resolved to give Rochester an extra-long walk that night to work off a few of those calories.

"I wonder why Joel Goldberg came to the temple last night," I said, after a couple of minutes. "Did he know that his brother wouldn't be there? Maybe he intended to vandalize the place? Leave some message for the men who tried to kick him out on Sunday?"

"You don't need a reason to do things when your brain doesn't work right."

"Did you ask the rabbi what kind of drugs his brother was supposed to be taking?"

He opened his notebook again and flipped back a couple of pages. "Thorazine, which lots of doctors prescribe to treat symptoms like hallucinations and delusions. But if he was homeless, then there was a solid chance he'd didn't have a way to refill his prescriptions and he went off his meds. I asked the coroner to run screens for common anti-psychotic drugs."

"The rabbi he said he didn't know that his brother was in the area," I said. "So what brought him here unannounced?"

"That's a big question," Rick said. "I pulled up Joel's police record. Last arrest was for vagrancy in Trenton, three weeks ago."

"So he's been in the area at least that long. But no contact with his brother. Where was he picked up?"

"Why does that matter?" "Dunno. Just curious."

"I think it was somewhere on Market Street. Mill Hill neighborhood?"

"My mother lived near there for a while when she was a child," I said. "Once as we were passing she pointed out this house with two red doors. Her father broke his leg when she was in elementary school, and they had to live somewhere on the first floor so he didn't have to climb steps."

"Is there a point to that stroll down memory lane?"

"Just that it was a Jewish neighborhood, back in the day. Maybe Joel was drawn there for some reason."

"More likely because there's a homeless shelter not far away," Rick said. "And that Mill Hill neighborhood is getting gentrified, bit by bit. Government workers buying houses there and renovating them."

"Panhandling targets?"

He nodded. "And there's still some crime of opportunity there. I have a friend who works over in Trenton. We get together and compare notes now and then."

We finished up, and Rick insisted on paying the tab. "Thanks for the conversation. I don't like to talk about this stuff with Tamsen. She has enough on her plate already."

I thought Rick was probably sheltering Tamsen too much, but didn't say anything. She had survived her soldier husband's death in Iraq, created a successful business, and raised her son by herself. She was strong enough, and smart enough, for Rick to confide in her. And this wasn't as upsetting a case as some he'd handled; Joel was a stranger, and the crime hadn't been overly gruesome. I wondered if he'd be able to open up more once they were committed and living together.

When I got home, Lili was pacing around the living room, which I assumed meant that the conversation with her brother had gone about as well as she expected. Fedi and Sara were reaching the end of their rope in dealing with Senora Weinstock and decisions would have to be made soon.

I went upstairs and climbed into bed with a book. Rochester followed me, sprawled sideways with one foot resting on my leg. Lili joined us a half hour later.

"Do you think our parents are ever happy with us?" she asked, as she sat on the bed beside me.

"You're asking me? The convicted felon? That was something my father bragged about, for sure."

"But he loved you. I can feel it in the stories you tell."

"He did, and my mother, too. I was very lucky that way. I only wish they were still here. They'd love you, and my dad would get a kick out of playing with Rochester."

"You miss them," Lili said.

"Of course. Not on a daily basis, you know, but when I hear something they said coming out of my mouth, or something triggers a memory. You miss your dad, don't you?"

"Oh, yes. He used to call me *mi nena bonita*, my pretty girl. He spoiled me, and my mother was the same way with Fedi. The sun shone on her little *papito*."

"And now your dad is gone, and you're stuck with your mom, knowing you weren't her favorite."

"It's not like that," Lili protested, though it was clear to me it was just like that. "She had different aspirations for each of us. She wanted me to get married, settle down and have babies. And that wasn't in the cards for me."

She sighed. "She's my mother. I love her. And she's always been huge on the subject of taking care of your parents. None of my grandparents wanted to leave Cuba, but after my mother's father died, my mother forced my *abuela* to come to Kansas City and live with us. She hated it, and she died only a few years later, but my mother always bragged that she had done what was right."

It sounded like a move Mary would have made, forcing an elderly woman to bend to her will. Lili was the opposite – she would do whatever made her mother happy. And that attitude was why I loved her.

We spent the rest of the evening lying beside each other, both of us reading but comforted by the proximity. Rochester repositioned himself at the end of the bed, keeping an eye on both of us.

Eventually we readied for bed, and as I turned out the lights, I said, "Tomorrow night I want to go to services at Shomrei Torah. I think the rabbi could use someone to talk about his brother with."

"I've been thinking about him, too, and how sad he must be about the loss of his brother," Lili said. "I liked the way he spoke at the blessing of the animals. And I could use a little spirituality myself. I think I'll join you."

We curled into each other. I may not have had much family left, I thought, but I had Lili and Rochester, and they were all I needed.

Chapter 10
Days of Awe

I spent most of the day Thursday with an Eastern faculty member who wanted to rent Friar Lake on behalf of an organization he was involved with, the National Council of Professors of Religion and Religious Thought. Felton Backus was in his fifties, with a mane of white hair and a matching beard. He could have doubled for Moses in one of those paintings of the parting of the Red Sea – just give him a staff he could raise up to summon God.

"We're organizing a retreat we're calling Religious Study and the New World Economy," he said. "And as you can imagine, the economy doesn't look favorably on small academic groups without a lot of money. I'm hoping we can get some kind of staff discount on the facilities."

"Let's figure out what you need and then I'll see what I can do on the price." Rochester accompanied us as I showed him around the property. "Religion is certainly a hot topic today," I said as we walked. "So much prejudice everywhere."

"It's one of the things we study in Introduction to World Religions," he said. "How people pervert religious doctrine to serve their own needs."

"I'm teaching a course in the English department on Jewish-

American literature this term." I told him about the section in the Cahan book about David Levinsky's study of the Torah. "That's the only truly religions element in what we've read so far, though. Most of the material we've read has more to do with assimilation."

"You can't ignore the connection, though," he said. "One of the complaints people have about Muslims these days is the visible way they connect with their religion, through the use of the head scarf or the burka. The argument is that they need to assimilate and adopt American customs. And that feeling often leads to cruelty and crime."

I remembered Joel Goldberg, and his assertion that the criminals of the Holocaust were still among us. Would we ever learn to get along with each other?

Professor Backus and I had a lively discussion as we looked at the rooms his group needed, and then we returned to my office and went over the rental agreement and discussed catering options.

"Can we bring in our own food to save money?" he asked. "Absolutely." He negotiated me down on everything he could,
from audio visual equipment to promising they'd set up and take down all their own chairs. By mid-afternoon we had hammered out an agreement and I was delighted to see his Volvo, adorned with liberal bumper stickers, head out of the parking lot.

I checked my voice mail as I walked Rochester around the property, and saw a message from Rick. He'd received the toxicology results on Joel Goldberg, and it appeared that there was no trace of any of the anti-psychotic drugs in his blood. That didn't mean he was experiencing an episode, but it increased the possibility.

By that afternoon, I was glad to be able to close Friar Lake up and head for home. I felt a vague sense of unease and I wasn't sure what to attribute it to. Was it the situation with Lili's mother? Or the death of Rabbi Goldberg's brother? Or something else entirely that had yet to percolate its way to the surface?

That evening, Lili spoke to her brother briefly, but then we shared the sofa, both of us reading until it was time for Rochester's late walk, and then bed. The next day at Friar Lake, I went through the discussion posts my lit students had made online, responding to a question I'd posed about ethnic literature in general. Was it a window into another culture? Or a way of ghettoizing the "other," those who were out of the mainstream, not yet assimilated?

The responses were very politically correct, to be expected of young people with a liberal education. How was I going to break through that veneer to get to what they really thought? I considered my conversation with Professor Backus and came up with a couple of new questions based on what he'd said about the connection between religion and assimilation.

Friday was a sluggish day and I was glad to shut down Friar Lake and head for home. After a quick dinner, Lili and I drove to the modern stone and glass temple building. I couldn't help looking toward the place where Joel Goldberg's body had been found. The police cones were long gone, as was any evidence that a murder had happened there. I shivered at how easily the evidence had disappeared.

I was on edge as we parked and walked inside, worried that she wouldn't enjoy the service, that she'd feel out of place because she didn't have the same roots I had there.

Daniel Epstein, one of the elderly men from Talmud study, was in the foyer outside the sanctuary, and I greeted him and introduced him to Lili. I was impressed that he was able to multi-task so well at his advanced age—handing out prayerbooks, wishing everyone Shabbat Shalom, while balancing on his silver-topped cane.

"What a beautiful space," Lili said, as we walked in. Early evening light streamed through the tall glass windows looking out at the nature preserve. A clerestory of stained glass cast multicolored shards on the wooden pews with their burgundy cushions. "It feels so warm and welcoming. I keep seeing angles I'd like to shoot it from."

I squeezed her hand. "I'm glad you like it."

The rabbi and cantor were already at the bema, preparing for the service, and Lili and I sat in a pew a few rows back. When the service started, she joined in whenever we recited from the prayer book, knew the words to some of the Hebrew and seemed to be enjoying herself.

As the cantor sang, I looked around the room. Was it possible that a member of the congregation, someone in the sanctuary, had killed Joel Goldberg? But what connection could he have to Shomrei Torah, other than that his brother led the worship there?

When the rabbi stepped up to the lectern for his sermon, he looked older than he had the previous Sunday, with a sadness in his face and a slight hunch to his shoulders.

He said some of the same things he'd spoken about at the Talmud study group – the way the old year was winding down, and we had to prepare to welcome the new one, and with it the introspection that came during the Days of Awe between Rosh Hashanah and Yom Kippur.

"This is a time to consider the sins of the previous year and repent before Yom Kippur. One of the common greetings at the time will be 'May you be inscribed in the Book of Life and sealed for a good year.'"

He looked out at the congregation. "We believe that God writes our names in this book on Rosh Hashanah, deciding who will have a good life in the new year, who will live and who will die. However, we have the ten days until Yom Kippur to change that decree, through acts of *teshuvah*, *tefilah* and *tzedakah* -- repentance, prayer, and good deeds. Then the books are sealed and our fate determined until the following Rosh Hashanah."

He took a deep breath. "Some of you may know that I lost my brother Joel this week. He suffered from mental illness, which made him difficult to love sometimes, and he will be in my thoughts during the Days of Awe. I hope that all of you will take this opportunity to let those you love know how you feel, to repair any old breaches and resolve to spend the next year in a state of joy with each other."

I reached over and squeezed Lili's hand once again. I could see in her face that she had been touched by the rabbi's words, and perhaps was thinking of her mother and her brother. I continued to hold her hand until we stood for the final prayers.

"What do you think of Shomrei Torah?" I asked, after we had sung the Adon Olam hymn together with the congregation, Lili's mezzo soprano joining with my tenor.

"It reminds me a lot of the synagogue we joined when it was time for Fedi's bar mitzvah. And I was moved by the rabbi's sermon."

At the Oneg Shabbat, the gathering for food and drink after the service, I introduced her to Rabbi Goldberg. She shook his hand and repeated how moved she had been by his sermon. "I have a brother myself," she said. "You've inspired me to be kinder in my dealings with him."

"It's music to a rabbi's ears to know that I've reached a congregant," he said. "I hope you'll continue to join us for worship now and then."

Then he turned to me and shook my hand. "Good to see you, Steve."

"How are you doing?" I asked him.

"Still very troubled. I've been praying for guidance. I keep looking at that photo the police found in Joel's shoe and wondering what it means."

I moved in closer to the rabbi so no one could overhear us. "Detective Stemper said your brother might have stayed at a homeless shelter in Trenton near where he was arrested for vagrancy a couple of weeks ago. You could go over there and see if anyone remembers him. If he said anything that indicated why he was looking for you, or some reason why he was holding onto that photo."

He took a deep breath. "I'm afraid of what I could find out," he said. "I don't know that I could face people who knew Joel, and the possibility that they'd judge me for abandoning him. I never felt that I had, you know. I just had to love him the best I could, and do what he'd let me do for him."

"I could go for you," I said, and I saw Lili shoot a glance at me. "Maybe as a disinterested party I could find out something that might help you feel better. And as you said, it's good to perform acts of kindness for others."

"I'd appreciate that very much," he said, and then someone wanted his attention.

"You just can't keep from sticking your nose into things, can you?" Lili said, as she laced her arm in mine. "But in this case I think you're doing a *mitzvah*. The poor man is hurting, and maybe you'll be able to find something to comfort him."

She stepped back from me then. "Just be careful."

Chapter 11
Rescue Mission

When we got home from services that evening, I was thinking about the conversation between Lili and the rabbi, how both of them had brothers. Growing up, I'd always wanted an older brother to show me the way, and I was envious of the relationship as boys that Rob and Joel Goldberg had shared, before Joel's illness manifested itself.

But the Bible reminded us that relationships with brothers weren't always smooth, didn't it? I realized that though I knew that Cain had killed his brother I didn't remember why. I got up and searched my bookcase until I found the embossed Bible I'd been given at my bar mitzvah, and looked up the section in Genesis.

Considering this was such an important and familiar story, the text in the Bible was pretty sparse. Cain and Abel both made offerings to the Lord, and while the Lord liked Abel's, he didn't like Cain's. So Cain got mad and killed Abel, presumably out of jealousy – a kind of "Dad likes you best" thing.

That couldn't be all, could it? I turned to my laptop and searched through the commentaries online. The best I could come up with was an interpretation that Abel sacrificed his best lamb to the Lord, while Cain burned some dried up wheat. That explained why God preferred Abel's offering, but it didn't satisfy me. Why would a benevolent creator favor one brother over the other, to the point of causing a murder? Didn't make God out to be that great a guy. I decided I'd have to ask Rabbi Goldberg the next time I saw him.

But then I stopped. Bringing up Cain and Abel so soon after the death of his own brother could be insensitive, maybe even suggest to him that I suspected him in Joel's death.

Could there have been something between Rob and Joel that pushed the rabbi to kill his brother? Rob wanted to keep the job at Shomrei Torah, and Joel threatened that. I couldn't reconcile the temperament that would lead someone to the rabbinate with that of a man who could kill his own brother in cold blood. And if that was the case, why kill Joel on the synagogue grounds, and leave his body there? It didn't make any sense.

I left the Bible on the coffee table in case I wanted to go back to it, and went upstairs to Lili. "What are you going to do to help the rabbi?" Lili asked, as I sat down on the bed beside her.

"Rick thought Joel might have been staying at a homeless shelter in Trenton," I said. "I'm going to drive over there tomorrow and see if that's true, and if anyone there remembers him."

"Just be careful," Lili said. "I don't want anything to happen to you." Rochester jumped up on the bed and walked right between us, where he settled down on his side, his legs toward me. She scratched behind his ears. "Or you either, sweetheart."

Saturday morning, I took Rochester for a long walk just after dawn. A wind had blown through the night before, and multi-colored leaves littered the ground. He was eager to stick his big nose into every pile and pee on it, and I had to keep reining him in.

Lili and I shared croissants and mugs of hot chocolate for breakfast, and after she left to meet Rick and go ring-shopping, I loaded Rochester into the car for the trip to Trenton. The memories began flooding past as we crossed the Scudder's Falls Bridge into New Jersey and began to drive south along the river. "This is my past, puppy," I said to him. "Not always a good thing to go digging through what's dead and buried, though, is it?"

He didn't respond, just stuck his head out the window as we passed Villa Victoria Academy, where I'd competed in speech and debate, mildly freaked out by the prevalence of crosses in the classrooms. Then we drove through the Jewish neighborhood of Hiltonia, where many of my mother's childhood friends had moved after leaving the center of town.

Even though we lived in the suburbs, we were still umbilically connected to the city across the river. As we drove it became clear that though I'd left Trenton, it hadn't left me. Decades had passed, but I still felt viscerally connected to the streets and landmarks. I remembered visiting family, attending Shomrei Torah before it moved to the suburbs, shopping at stores my mother had patronized since she was a girl.

So many landmarks had disappeared, most of them demolished in the name of urban renewal that the streets hardly looked familiar anymore. The house with the two red doors I'd mentioned to Rick had been replaced by a state office building. The old Sinclair gas station with its dinosaur statue out front was long gone, along with the bakery where I got an ice cream birthday cake every year.

I wondered how Rob and Joel Goldberg had celebrated their birthdays as kids. Did they share, squabble? I'd wanted a brother to play with when I was a lonely only child, tagging along behind my parents to adult events.

After driving a few minutes, I realized I had no idea how to get to the Rescue Mission, the homeless shelter Rick had mentioned. I looked up the address on my phone and plugged it into my GPS, which directed me to a four-story old brick warehouse in downtown Trenton, only a few blocks from where the fancy stores used to be on State Street. I parked in the adjacent lot, put Rochester on his leash and warned him to be on his best behavior.

When I walked in the foyer, the largest man I'd ever seen in real life stood in front of me, at least six-five, with huge shoulders, chest and belly. He held two men apart by the backs of their shirts. "No fighting here. You got that?"

He looked at the guy on his left, who said, "Yeah." Then the guy on his right said the same thing. The big guy let them go, and they walked off in opposite directions. He dusted off his hands and looked at me. "Afternoon. How can I help you?"

I introduced myself and made sure it was okay to have Rochester with me.

"We can have dogs visit, but not stay overnight."

"That's okay, I'm not here to check in." Rochester slumped to the floor beside me. "I'm interested in a guy who might have come through here in the past couple of weeks. White, early thirties, brown hair. Diagnosed with paranoid schizophrenia."

Something like recognition flickered on Buddha's face. "You a cop?"

"Not at all. This gentleman died on Wednesday night, en route to see his brother, Rabbi Rob Goldberg of Shomrei Torah in Stewart's Crossing. The rabbi's very upset, as you can imagine, and he asked me to track his brother's movements to see if I can find out what he wanted from the rabbi."

"So you're a private investigator?"

Rochester sat up. Maybe he was a private detective, but I wasn't. How could I explain why the rabbi had asked me to do this? I went for the simplest explanation. "Just a friend of the rabbi's. He's too upset to do this himself, so he asked me to."

The big man accepted that. "Buddha McCarthy," he said, and he stuck out his hand for me to shake. It was so big that my hand felt puny in his. Then he turned to Rochester, and petted his head. Rochester opened his mouth and grinned.

"You're the peacekeeper around here?" I asked Buddha. "Among other things. I manage the shelter so my size is an
   advantage."

He nodded his head toward an open door behind him. "I remember the guy you're asking about. Joel, right?" I nodded.

"Come into the office with me and I'll dig up the information we have on him."

Rochester and I followed him into a small room with lots of small photos on the white walls, of individuals and events. "Your success stories?" I asked, pointing at them.

"Some of them. Some couldn't make it no matter how hard they tried, or we did. So I keep their pictures up there, too, to remind me." He sat down behind the desk, and I sat across from him, with Rochester on the floor beside me.

"What happened to Joel?" he asked.

"He went out to the synagogue in Stewart's Crossing and someone killed him before he could see his brother," I said. "Blow to the head with a blunt object."

Buddha sighed. "It's a tough world out there. A lot of these folks are sick, or they have mental problems, or they're ex-cons."

"Tell me about it," I said. "I did a year in California for computer hacking. If I hadn't had the support of a couple of good people I might have ended up here myself."

"No, I can tell by looking at you. White, smart, good attitude. You'd have made it."

I was flattered, but I believed that if it hadn't been for people like Lucas Roosevelt and Rick Stemper, I would have floundered, no matter my skin color or my intelligence level. And as for a good attitude, well, my parole officer would have disagreed with that. Despite his best efforts over the two years I had been assigned to him, I still hadn't kicked my addiction to hacking, and I wasn't sure I ever would.

Buddha opened a big logbook. "We keep a record of everybody who comes in," he said. "We need it for legal purposes, as well as to show the people who fund us what kind of work we're doing. You can see from how short the lists are that it's been quiet for a while— not too hot or too cold, so a lot of folks have been living rough." He motioned out the window, where gray clouds were massing. "Supposed to pour tonight, so we should get a few extra folks."

He flipped through the pages, and I had to hold Rochester back, because he wanted to look, too. "Joel showed up here about week ago Thursday. It was a rainy day, and I remember he looked like a drowned rat. We got him dried out, washed his clothes, that kind of thing. At the time he didn't show any signs of mental illness – he was very polite, well-spoken, apologetic."

Was he still under the influence of his medications at the time?

Or simply not yet in the grip of an episode?

Buddha closed his eyes, and I could see that childhood resemblance to his namesake remained. He exuded a kind of quiet warmth that I was sure many of the clients at the shelter responded well to.

When he opened them again, he said, "Joel said that he was looking for old records of Trenton, like lists of people who lived here back in the day. I sent him to the library down the street, and he stayed with us for a couple of days, doing well, spending lots of time with whatever research he was doing. But then last Saturday he appeared to be going into a manic phase. Talking non-stop, rambling about the Holocaust. His grandparents, who escaped, and some other man who didn't—but then somehow he did, and he showed up in Trenton."

Buddha sighed. "I have to admit I couldn't pay much attention because we were busy, and it didn't make a lot of sense."

Rochester got up and stretched, then began to nose around Buddha's office. I watched as he nosed at a photo of a man and two young boys, and I remembered the photo postcard that had been found folded up in Joel's shoe.

"Did Joel mention the names Aaron or Kalman while he was here?"

"Not that I remember. Family members?"

As I explained about the picture of the two boys, Rochester slumped back beside me.

"He told me he'd been hanging around the ruins of this old

temple. There were still a couple of walls up and he was sheltering there, said he could still feel the religious vibrations. Maybe he found the picture there."

"You know where it is?"

"No idea." He sighed. "Sunday morning he got into a scrap with another guy. He was one of these neo-Nazi types, shaved head and a swastika tattooed on his wrist, and when Joel saw that he went kind of ape-shit."

"Did they fight?"

"They both got a couple of punches in before I could pull them apart. Joel grabbed his stuff and got out, and the skinhead, who gave his name as John White, left that night. Neither of them came back since."

"When you say 'gave his name as' – you don't think that was his real name?"

"I doubt it. A lot of our residents don't have ID so we accept what they say."

I wrote down Rick's name and phone number and handed it to Buddha. "If this White guy comes back, can you call the detective who's investigating Joel's death?"

He looked at the piece of paper, which seemed tiny in his giant hand. "If he comes back."

Had this guy run into Joel again? What if their argument had erupted once more? But what would a skinhead with a swastika tattoo be doing at Shomrei Torah? Could Joel have interrupted him preparing to deface the building, and gotten killed while defending his brother's temple? Maybe Joel had been angry at his brother, and somehow recruited this skinhead to help?

They both seemed pretty far-fetched, but I had to consider them as possibilities.

"A real shame about Joel," Buddha said. "But I can't say I'm surprised. We see a fair number of mentally ill folks here, and there's rarely a happy ending for them."

I thanked Buddha for his help and left him my card in case he thought of anything else. As I walked back to the car, I called Rick and told him about John White.

"That's a good lead," he said. "I'll call the other shelters in the area and see if he's shown up anywhere else. And I'll call this McCarthy guy and see if he can give me a better description, particularly of the tattoo. Guy like that, he probably has a record somewhere."

I hung up and looked down at Rochester. "Thanks for reminding me about the photograph, boy," I said, and I scratched behind his ears. "You want to see if we can find this place where Joel was squatting?"

He looked up at me with his doggy grin, his tongue lolling out of his mouth, and I figured that was a yes.

It began to drizzle as I walked Rochester over to a stand of trees for a quick pee. When we got back to the car, he settled on the front seat beside me and I wondered if Joel had been squatting at the old home of Shomrei Torah, where I'd had my bar mitzvah.

When my grandparents first arrived in Trenton in the early part of the twentieth century, they lived in a neighborhood near the Delaware called Jewtown, a warren of narrow streets where Yiddish was the *lingua franca*. In the 1960s, urban renewal had swept much of the area away, replacing it with a complex of government buildings and a highway linking the city and the suburbs.

Though I'd been to the old shul a thousand times in my childhood, it took some navigating to find it again, and Rochester sat beside me on the front seat, eagerly peering out the window. The building didn't look much like what I remembered, and I felt my heart pierced. Most of the simple structure of white stone had been demolished, in preparation for the construction of a convenience store. The entire front wall was gone, and with it the double doors beneath a semi-circular stained glass window of a six-pointed Star of David.

Gone too were the two tall stained glass windows that had flanked the door and the triangular pediment above those. All that remained was the wall along the right side, a few feet of the rear wall, and a bit of roof above them. I could see how Joel Goldberg might have found shelter there.

The rain had stopped spitting, so Rochester and I got out of the car. The warehouse building across the street was shuttered, the lots on either side empty. There was no one around to tell us we couldn't snoop, so we did.

We walked up to the covered space, and I saw signs that someone had been living there—a couple of fast food wrappers, a used condom, and an empty beer bottle. I looked around as much as I could but I couldn't find anything that connected to Joel Goldberg, or that indicated if he'd found the photograph there.

Rochester kept straining to go to the Belgian block wall along the rear of the property. Those rectangular blocks, in shades of gray and purple, had been brought to the new world as ballast in ships, and then used for building. I knew about them because my father had collected them, using them to build the lakefront wall behind our house.

When I was a kid, there was an old wall, like the one behind the shul, on an empty lot on the way to my grandmother's house in Trenton. My father would often stop if he saw one of the blocks had come loose and he'd retrieve it and take it home with us. I never thought anything of it at the time, but of course it was theft. Maybe I came by my criminal tendencies honestly.

I let Rochester lead me over to the wall, where he sniffed at one of the blocks and then sat on his haunches in front of it. He raised his right paw to the block, and it wobbled. "Something behind there?" I asked him. I grabbed the block and was surprised at how easily it came loose. Shades of my father, I thought.

Behind the block a spot had been hollowed out in the dirt. A small metal box, of the kind I used to keep three by five cards in, rested inside. I looked around. A couple of cars passed on the street, but there was no one nearby. I reached in and pulled the box out.

With Rochester trying to nose his way in, I opened the box. I opened the box without considering I'd be leaving fingerprints. There was a single piece of yellowed paper inside, folded many times. It was written in Hebrew, but even after all the years studying the language in preparation for my bar mitzvah, my Hebrew was limited to prayers and the occasional phrase remembered from dusty afternoons where our teachers used picture books about Israeli children to school us in conjugating verbs.

I stared at the heading on the page because I felt like I ought to recognize it. Hebrew reads from right to left, and the left-most character was the *yod*, which looked like an apostrophe and represented the letter Y. The next letter was the *dalet*, or D. That word I knew – it was "yad," which meant "hand," and also was the name of the pointer used when reading from the Torah.

The next letter, a straight line with a sort of curlicue at the top, was the *vav*, the letter V. Then the *shin*, the "sh" sound, and the *mem*, the M. Vishim? Vashem? Va-shem. Of course. Yad Vashem was the Holocaust memorial site in Israel.

That tied in to what both Buddha and Rabbi Goldberg had said—that Joel was interested in something relating to the Holocaust. Had whatever he'd found pushed him into a manic phase? Or was it just that he'd stopped taking his meds?

Had there been more in the box? The photo of the two boys, for instance? And if Joel had taken that, why would he have left this document behind? Because he couldn't read it? Or perhaps there had been an English translation with it, that he had taken, and then lost?

I replaced the Belgian block, grabbed the box and Rochester's leash, and hot-footed it back to my car. I'd gone to prison once and wasn't eager to get picked up for petty theft.

Chapter 12
Se Habla Yiddish

As soon as I got home, I opened my laptop and turned to Google Translate. Using a virtual Hebrew keyboard, I typed in a few words from the paper I'd found behind the Belgian block, but I got no results that made any sense.

I sat back and looked over at Rochester. "It's like hieroglyphics," I said to him. "I need something to help me figure out what stands for what. You didn't find a Rosetta Stone near that worry stone, did you?"

He hopped up on my lap, his big tail wagging over the coffee table in front of me, and he knocked the Bible I'd left there to the floor. Some atavistic impulse told me to dust it off and kiss it, and as I did I remembered the practice of either pressing your prayer book, or the fringe of your tallis, against the Torah as the rabbi paraded it around the sanctuary at the end of the weekly Torah service.

"The rabbi has to speak Hebrew," I said to Rochester. "I'll call him tomorrow and have him translate." I rubbed my hand over the soft top of his head. "Good boy. Good clue."

A short time later, Lili returned like a successful hunter with news about the ring Rick had chosen. "It's exactly what I was looking for," she said. "An oval-cut, one-carat emerald in a white gold setting with a diamond baguette on each side."

I couldn't help but hear the "what I was looking for." Was this some kind of big hint as to what kind of engagement ring she wanted? That she wanted to get engaged?

Before I could obsess too much, she continued, "I think it's what Tamsen will like. Not something I'd wear—too traditional."

"Mary's was very contemporary," I said, relieved that she'd deflected my unasked question, and giving me the chance to indulge my curiosity. "Did you have engagement rings from either of your marriages?"

"Not from Adriano, just a narrow gold band when we got married. Philip insisted on a big ring, like I was a trophy he could show off. A circle of diamonds and sapphires. I sold it as soon as the divorce was final and used the money for air fare to Tanzania to try my hand at photojournalism. I swore I'd never wear a ring like that again."

I waited a couple of beats, but when she didn't say anything more, I knew I had to plunge in. "Does that mean you never want an engagement ring, or that you never want to get married again?" I asked. "I know we've talked about this before, but I want to make sure we're still on the same page."

She cocked her head and looked at me, and then burst out laughing. "Did you think I was hinting that I want a ring from you?"

I nodded, though I didn't understand why she was laughing. "Oh, sweetie," she said, and she leaned forward and kissed me.

"You know I'm not the shy type. If I change my mind about getting married, you'll be the first to know." Then she pulled back. "You haven't changed, have you?"

I shook my head. "I love you and I want to be with you. I don't need a bunch of legal paperwork for that."

"And we both know how awful it is to go through divorce. So we're good?"

"We're better than good," I said, smiling. "Great. Awesome. Outrageously wonderful."

Maybe it was my visit to the old shul that morning, but I thought that if Lili and I ever did get married, I'd want a Jewish ceremony, preferably in a synagogue. Lili's family, and the remains of my own, a few distant cousins, there to witness our commitment.

It all came back to family, didn't it? The legacy my parents and grandparents had left me in Trenton and Stewart's Crossing, Lili's issues with her mother, the rabbi's loss of his brother. At least there was one of those I could do something about.

Lili's phone trilled, and she groaned. "That's Fedi," she said. "*Dios mio*, I can't believe he's calling me again. We just hung up an hour ago."

She picked up her phone and answered in Spanish. After a moment or two of spirited conversation, in which I only understood a few words, she hung up.

"My mother fell," she said. "It looks like she fractured her pelvis."

"Oh my," I said. "The poor woman."

"I can't keep doing this remotely. I told Fedi I'll fly down there tomorrow morning," she said. "I'll get someone to cover my classes. Can you drive me to the airport?"

"Of course. You don't want me to go with you?"

"Trust me, this isn't the way you want to meet my mother."

I ran out to DeLorenzo's for hoagies while Lili worked the phone, setting up her flight, her rental car, and her substitutes. I felt bad that I couldn't go with her, but I understood that this was something she had to do herself. We ate our sandwiches at the kitchen table, brainstorming things she had to do before she could leave, and questions she needed to ask once she was in Florida.

The situation made me wonder who would take care of Lili and me when we were old? Lili was a couple of years older than I was, but typically women lived longer than men. Both my parents had died young, too, which I guessed made me statistically likely to pass before

Lili did. So assuming we were still together, she'd take care of me. But what about her? Would she be able to rely on her brother, her niece and nephew?

"Do you have one of those living wills?" I asked, as we walked upstairs so that she could pack.

"I'm not my mother, Steve. I have a long way to go before I end up like her."

"You never know. Look at all the people we know who died young. I'm just saying, I think we should have those. I had a will made up once Rochester came to live with me, because I wanted to make sure he was taken care of. I should change that now."

I looked at her. "You'd keep him if anything happened to me, wouldn't you?"

"So he can drag me around to crime scenes?" She smiled. "Of course I will, *mi amor*. And you're right, we should both have up-to-date wills. We'll take care of that when I come home."

I kissed her, and because he knew we'd been talking about him, Rochester nosed between us, looking for love.

I sat on the bedroom floor with him, rubbing his belly and telling him he was a good boy, as Lili packed. He and I went out for our late evening walk, and by the time we returned Lili was already in bed.

I stripped down and slid beside her. "I'll miss you," I said, kissing her cheek. "Just remember. *Illegitimi non carborundum.*"

She laughed. "No, I won't let the bastards grind me down. Though if my mother or my brother knew you were calling them bastards they'd have words for you."

"Why I said it in Latin," I said. We curled into each other and Lili gave me something to remember her by – as if I needed the reminder. But I wasn't complaining.

The next morning we hurried through a dozen last minute things before we could leave for the airport. "You'll take those papers I was grading into my office so the students can pick them up?" Lili asked.

"Yes, love. You've already asked me that twice. And I'll call the dentist Monday and reschedule your checkup. I have the ticket for the dry cleaner's so I'll pick up your dress." "I'm sorry, I'm feeling a bit frantic."

"Don't worry. Focus on helping your mother."

"But what can I really do for her in a couple of days? We'll argue and she'll play the martyr and nothing will change."

"Don't be silly. You're going to talk to her doctors and you and Fedi will figure out exactly what's wrong with her and what you can do to make her comfortable and speed up her healing. I'm sure she'll feel better having you there."

I carried her bag out to the car and put it in the trunk, then opened the back door for Rochester. Lili slid into the front seat, then said, "*Coño!* Did I bring the keys to my mother's apartment?"

She patted her pockets. "Yes. They're here. Let's get on the road before I have a nervous breakdown."

Rochester nosed forward from the back seat, sniffing her shoulder, and she turned to pet him as we sped down the highway. "Thank God everything is digital now," she said. "My boarding pass and the email confirming my rental car are both on my phone. I'm pretty sure I remember how to get to her apartment but I can put the address into the GPS."

We talked about how much easier our lives were now that we didn't have to fret about carrying so much paperwork with us, and Lili seemed to relax.

When I pulled up in the drop-off lane at the airport, I kissed her goodbye and told her to call me whenever she needed to vent. And then, as I drove back up the highway, I felt a weird sense of freedom— I was single again, if only briefly, and my time was my own

– and Rochester's, of course. Everyone, even those happily coupled, liked a little private time, didn't they?

Not that I wouldn't miss Lili – I had grown accustomed to sharing my life with her, to discussing our days over dinner, to walking the dog with her sometimes, to fitting together in a hundred small ways. But it was going to be fun to be on my own for a few days, doing just what I wanted when I wanted, eating fast food without worrying about calories, having a second beer after dinner if I chose.

What did I want to do? I could go back home and get started on the to-do list Lili had left me—but instead I called Rabbi Goldberg. I wanted to show him the paper written in Hebrew that I'd found at the old shul and see what he could make of it.

He said that he'd be in his office for the next few hours, so Rochester and I stopped at the house to pick up the paper and then drove to Shomrei Torah, where we found the rabbi and Sadie in his office. While the dogs played together, I showed the rabbi the sheet and explained where I'd found it. I still didn't understand where it had come from, and how Joel, who wasn't a Trenton native, had stumbled on it.

He looked at it for a couple of minutes, his brow knotted in concentration. "This isn't Hebrew," he said after a while. "Though it's in the Hebrew alphabet, it's Yiddish. My parents were first generation Americans and they were determined to be assimilated. Joel and I almost never heard Yiddish at home, so I'm sure he couldn't make anything out of it, either."

"My dad's parents spoke to him in Yiddish and he answered in Yiddish, so he was pretty fluent. My mom could understand, but she'd always answered her parents in English. They only spoke Yiddish when they didn't want me to understand, so all I know of the language is a few colorful curses. Do you know anyone who could translate this?"

"Daniel Epstein probably could," he said. "Do you remember him from Talmud study? The elderly man who walks with a cane?"

"Sure. He's the one who was so sweet to Rochester. Could you call and ask him?"

He did, and Mr. Epstein extended an invitation to Rochester and me to come over to his house and show him the paper.

"I appreciate what you're doing, Steve. I feel like I'm getting closer to Joel with every detail you find."

"Have you been able to make funeral arrangements?" I asked.

He nodded. "Joel's body was released by the medical examiner yesterday afternoon. My parents want him to be buried near them, in Scottsdale, so the body will be shipped there today. I'm flying out this afternoon and we'll have the funeral tomorrow."

"Your parents must be very upset."

"They are. It's hard to lose a child—I've counseled many parents through that. But we all have to believe that Joel will be at peace now."

He thanked me again, and I led Rochester back out to the car and plugged Daniel Epstein's address into my phone, reminded as I did that Lili would be doing the same thing once she landed in Miami.

The directions led me down toward the river, on the other side of Stewart's Crossing from River Bend. Epstein lived in Crossing Estates, a development of large homes on what had been farmland when I was growing up.

I parked in the driveway on an imposing two-story in a faux Tudor style, and he appeared at the front door, leaning on the burnished wood cane I'd seen him use at the rabbi's study.

He greeted Rochester first, sticking his hand out for my golden to sniff, then petting him. "I wish I could have another dog," he said. "But I can't manage the walking."

"Thanks for agreeing to look at this paper," I said as he led us into a two-story foyer with a staircase in front of us. On the wall I noted a couple of framed sepia-toned photographs of the area where my grandparents had lived when they came to Trenton. "That's New Street, isn't it?" I asked, looking at one photo.

"You recognize it?"

"My great-uncle had a junkyard there. It was gone by the time I was born, but we had some old pictures. Nothing as nice as these, though."

"I took these pictures myself," Epstein said proudly. "When I was in college, for a history project. I found them a few years ago, had them blown up and framed. Always good to remember where we come from."

I agreed with that as I looked around the house. "You have a beautiful home."

"I love it," he said. "My children want me to sell it and move somewhere more manageable, but I'm not quite there yet. I have a bedroom and a full bath on this level, and I rarely climb the stairs anymore."

Rochester and I followed him into the living room, where the walls were lined with so much art that it reminded me of pictures I'd seen of Gertrude Stein's salon. I recognized an Andy Warhol of green Coca-Cola bottles, what looked like a Rothko with big blobs of color, and a couple of photo-realist works I knew Lili would love.

Epstein motioned me to an overstuffed armchair and sat at a small antique desk, with the paper in front of him.

As he pulled out a pair of reading glasses, I noticed a postcard beside his desk, what looked like a sign from a store in a tropical location. It read "Se habla Yiddish," and even I could get the joke. Must have been Miami, where Hispanics and Jews melded. The card was a good sign—I hoped it meant that Mr. Epstein had a real familiarity with the language.

While he read, Rochester sprawled on the floor beside him. "Hmm, hmm," Epstein said. Then he looked up at me. "This is a documentation form for Yad Vashem. You know what that is?"

"The Holocaust center in Israel?"

"The largest collection of Holocaust documentation in the world. Volunteers used to go to people in the resettlement camps after the war, and to survivors, and ask them to fill out forms about their family and friends and neighbors, who was lost in the Shoah and who was saved. Where did you find this?"

I explained about the metal box behind the Belgian block wall. "Any indication who wrote the document?" I asked.

"Myer Hafetz, native of Berlin, Germany."

Had Joel Goldberg's family come from Berlin? I'd have to ask the rabbi. "Is there any indication of who hid it there? Or a reason why someone would have hidden it?"

"I can't speculate without translating the whole document. I can do that for you, if you like."

"I'd appreciate that. Maybe one of the names will trigger something."

He made a photocopy of the document and returned the original to me. He wasn't big on using email, so I gave him my mailing address, and he promised to mail the translation to me in the next couple of days.

It was strange to return home with Rochester and not have Lili there to meet us. The house seemed emptier somehow. How had I lived on my own at first, and then with Rochester, before she had joined us?

To stave off any loneliness, I called Rick and invited him to bring Rascal over. I made a big pan of lasagna and put it in the oven.

Since many immigration records had been digitized, I wondered if I could find anything on line about Myer Hafetz. He was from Berlin, Epstein had said, and I knew that Hafetz had to be in Trenton by September 1948, when the document was dated.

The National Archives included many immigration records for arrivals to the United States from foreign ports between approximately 1820 and 1982, but they were all on microfilm. I had to go to one of the ancestry sites for online records, and there were way too many places to look and too little information to narrow a search.

I made a couple of quick tries but then Lili called and I gave up. "It's chaos here," she said. "My mother is very agitated, and Fedi and Sara are worn out, so it's all on me."

"I wish I could be there to help out," I said.

"She's supposed to have an oxygen mask on but she keeps pulling it off. She just keeps rambling in a weird combination of Spanish and Yiddish," she said. "I have no idea what she's saying most of the time."

I felt bad for Lili, and guilty at the same time. My mother had gotten sick when I was living in California, right after my ex-wife's first miscarriage. I had to be there for Mary, and I didn't realize my mother would pass so quickly. And then my father had gone into his decline while I was in prison, and I even had to miss his funeral. I hadn't been able to be there for either of them, and I couldn't do or say anything to damage Lili's relationship with her mother and lead her to the same kind of feelings I had.

I could, perhaps, do something for Joel Goldberg, and his brother. We'd see.

Chapter 13
Agitation

Rick and Rascal arrived a short while later. "Any news on the death of the rabbi's brother?" I asked, after I'd given him a beer and Rascal and Rochester both got treats.

"I tracked down the driver of the bus that night," he said. "The regular driver was sick and he was filling in. He thinks he remembers a homeless-looking guy get on at the train station, and then getting off at the synagogue. He does remember that two guys got off there, but couldn't identify a photo of Joel Goldberg. He wasn't paying attention, just wanted to finish the run and go home."

"Someone else got off at the synagogue with Joel. Maybe this other guy saw something."

"If I trust this driver's memory. There are a couple of developments within walking distance of that bus stop, so it could have been some guy on his way home. I'm going to meet the bus tomorrow night and see if maybe this guy is a regular, and if he or anyone else saw anything that night."

He sighed. "I don't have much to go on, and the chief is not happy. There hasn't been much in the press beyond a single mention in the Courier-Times, but because this is a township crime, he's getting pressure from over there, as well as from our side. It's possible that someone meant to rob the temple, and Joel got in the way. Which means there could be a burglar slash killer loose in town. No one likes that idea."

I served up the lasagna, and as we ate I told him what Daniel Epstein had said about the paper I'd found at the synagogue. "He says it's written in Yiddish, a lot of names. He's going to translate it for me and mail it back to me."

"There's no indication that Joel could understand Yiddish, is there?"

I shook my head. "Rabbi Rob says their parents didn't speak it to them."

"So it's unlikely that could have set him off, isn't it?" Rick said. "What about the photograph? Aaron is a pretty common name, I guess, but what about the other one – Kalman?"

"I don't think it's that popular," I said. "But we can look it up." I got my laptop and did a search for the name. Kalman was a Yiddish given name that came from the Hebrew, and farther back from Greek. It was also a Hungarian name given to children to ward off evil spirits. It had never been a popular first name.

"Can you search anywhere else?" Rick asked. "I mean, legally?" "Sure. I can go into some of the immigration databases. Maybe I can find a pair of brothers named Aaron and Kalman."

I sat back in my chair. "I think Joel Goldberg saw something that upset him in the ruins of the old synagogue," I said. "It made him agitated and sent him off to see his brother."

"That's one theory," Rick said. "But remember, the guy was schizophrenic. We don't know what was going on in his brain. He could just as easily have gone there to confront his brother, accuse him of something. I'm still not letting the rabbi off the hook, since he has no alibi for the time of Joel's death."

"Blaming the rabbi doesn't feel right." I didn't want to believe that Rabbi Goldberg had killed his brother – but there was the story of

Cain and Abel again, and I couldn't ignore the possibility. "And speaking of feelings, Lili told me that you picked out a ring for Tamsen."

His face brightened. "Yeah, it's a real stunner. I think she's going to love it."

"When are you going to give it to her?"

"I was thinking about when I propose," he said drily. "That's not what I meant, numb nuts."

"Not sure yet. I mean, I know I want to do it, but I want the time to be right. I want it to be special, you know?"

We brainstormed about places and times for a couple of minutes as we played with the dogs, but nothing jumped out at either of us. Eventually Rick and Rascal left, and then, as I had promised Rick, I spent some time online searching through immigration and family history records for a pair of German boys named Aaron and Kalman. The sheer volume of records was overwhelming. So many refugees fleeing the conflict in Europe, running from pogroms and other persecution. As I expected, Kalman wasn't that common a name, but none of the ones I found had a brother, or even a male cousin, named Aaron.

I spoke to Lili again late that night, just before bedtime. She'd had a confrontation with her sister-in-law Sara, who demanded to know if Lili had a copy of her mother's will.

"I was stunned," Lili said. "It's a broken pelvis, and it's serious, but it's not like she's going to die tomorrow. And the way Sara said it was like she thought I was conniving with my mother to inherit everything. It's not like I haven't gone down there before."

"There isn't that much, is there? Just her condo?"

"My dad was a very successful engineer," she said. "He made a lot of money and watched every penny he spent. She probably has a couple hundred thousand squirreled away. I don't need it and I don't mind if she leaves everything to Fedi and his kids. But I did not like the accusing tone Sara was using."

"I'm sure she's stressed," I said. "You said yourself that the burden of caring for your mother had fallen on her and Fedi."

"Burden," Lili said. "Hah. Until she fell, my mother has been pretty self-sufficient. Sure, she gets these obsessions and Fedi or Sara has to go over and calm her down, but she hasn't had trouble walking or taking care of herself. It's just Fedi who's been pushing her to move in with him."

"Trying to prevent this kind of problem?" "Whose side are you on, Steve?"

"Always yours, sweetheart. Remember what I said last night? Don't let them grind you down."

"I'm tired and cranky. I'll talk to you tomorrow."

We ended the call with mutual affirmations of love and I went to bed, Rochester eager to take Lili's place by my side.

Monday was a slow day at Friar Lake, and it gave me a lot of time to think about Lili and hope that her mother would improve quickly so she could come home. Rochester sensed my grim mood and brought me his squeaky ball. He dropped it at my feet and looked up at me with his doggy grin. I picked up the ball, which was slippery with saliva, then immediately brushed my hand against my pants. "Come on, boy, let's go outside and play," I said, and he romped out of my office, his tail wagging madly.

I called him the golden thiever because he didn't usually like to play fetch; he'd get the ball or Frisbee or whatever I'd thrown and then settle down with it firmly clasped between his paws. But that afternoon he was willing to play, and I threw the ball several times in the grassy yard beside my office.

The leaves on the oaks beside the abbey chapel had begun to turn, and there was a crispness in the air that presaged autumn. But I couldn't stay melancholy because Rochester's joy was so infectious.

I spent some time online looking for information about Joel Goldberg. I used a couple of different search engines and a combination of terms, and I found a lot of material. Over the past year, Joel had been a frequent poster to a Holocaust information list serve, mentioning occasionally that he had to rely on public internet access at libraries and cafés, and he engaged in many discussions about how to trace family members and others who had died during the Shoah.

In my conversation with the rabbi, he'd mentioned that their grandparents had survived the camps, and through Joel's posts I discovered it was their father's parents that he'd been talking about. Lev and Rifka Goldberg had been children in Auschwitz for a short time before they were liberated. Joel had apparently pored over many lists of inmates, both those who died and those who survived, looking for their names and those of any family members.

He had been constricted by the common nature of his last name. Many families from Russia, Poland and Germany shared it, and according to what he'd written, Joel didn't know the name of the village his grandparents had come from. Some of the databases he mentioned were private, either by subscription or membership, and I resisted the impulse to hack my way into them. Joel didn't seem to have much of a filter in his messages and posts; if he had learned something I was sure it would be online in a public place. I wasn't sure if that was naiveté on his part, a side effect of his illness—or just an innocence of the kind of trouble that openness could bring.

There was way too much material, and I didn't have enough information to know what I was looking for, so eventually I gave up. I sat at my desk, staring into space, when Rochester came up to me, wagging his tail, with a book in his mouth that he'd picked up from the coffee table in the lobby. "Did you want me to read to you, puppy?" I asked, as I pried the book from his jaws. It was a copy of the coffee table book Lili and I had collaborated on about the history of Friar Lake. She'd taken gorgeous photos of the exteriors and interiors of the old stone buildings, both before and after renovation, and I'd written text about the history of the property.

Rochester sat up and stared at me.

"What? You can't want to go out. We just went."

I looked at the book in my hand. Was he trying to tell me something about the abbey? About Lili?

I hefted the book in my hand, getting a sense memory of all those days I'd ferried books home from the old Gothic-style library in Stewart's Crossing.

Of course. The library. Buddha McCarthy at the Rescue Mission had told me that he'd sent Joel Goldberg to the library in Trenton to look up old records. "You think I ought to go to the library, don't you, boy?" I asked, and Rochester woofed.

We left Friar Lake soon after that. It was a hot day by autumn standards and I didn't want to leave Rochester in the car, so I dropped him at home, gave him a biscuit, and promised I'd be back soon.

I used my phone to locate the library branch closest to the Rescue Mission and drove along the river through Yardley and then Morrisville, and across the Calhoun Street Bridge into Trenton, taking another of my nostalgic journeys into my past. I recognized the building as I parked nearby – a two-story marble building with big windows and a four-columned entrance portico. Back when I was a kid, my mother had held onto her Trenton library card, and she'd taken me there a couple of times while she looked for something and I got to browse through the kids' books.

The librarian at the reference desk, a hipster guy with tattoos and a goatee, remembered Joel. The plaque in front of him said that his name was Akiva Teitelboim, a classic Jewish name, but surprisingly he had a light Spanish accent.

"He was very well-spoken for a homeless guy," he said. "We get a lot of the homeless looking for shelter here when it rains or gets too cold."

"You remember what he was looking for?"

"First off, he wanted a phone book, and then I saw him looking through the bus schedules over there." He pointed to a rack of brochures listing each route.

The need for bus schedules was evident, if Joel was on his way to Shomrei Torah. "Anything else?" I asked the librarian.

"He asked if we had anything about the history of Trenton from the 1940s, and I told him about our Trentoniana collection. We have a huge collection of photographs, manuscripts, trade cards, letters, postcards, diaries and maps. Lots of old newspapers on microfilm, too."

What could Joel have been looking for in the historical archive? As far as I knew, the Goldbergs hadn't lived in Trenton in the 1940s. Did his search have something to do with the photo of the two boys that had been in his shoe?

"Why are you looking for him? Did he do something wrong?"

I shook my head. "He was killed at the synagogue a few days ago, and his brother wants to understand what he was doing here."

He wanted to know who had killed his brother, too, but that wasn't why I'd come to the library.

"That's sad," Akiva said. "There's one more thing. He recognized my name as Jewish, and asked me if I was named after Rabbi Akiba from the Bible. And if I was, why was my name spelled with a V instead of a B."

"I assume you are," I said. Something in my brain clicked. "Are you from South America?"

"I was born in Argentina. My great-grandparents came from various parts of Poland and Russia, and when they were fleeing the Holocaust they couldn't get into the US. So they landed in Buenos Aires. There was a bombing at the Jewish Community Center where I went to nursery school, so my parents decided to pick up and move here."

Akiva frowned. "I told him a little bit about my family history, which turned out to be a big mistake. He started rambling about how he knew that there were Nazis, or Nazi sympathizers, living among us. That he had come to Trenton to warn his brother, who's a rabbi."

"I've spoken to his brother," I said. "We've been trying to figure out why Joel came to Trenton in the first place, so that fills in a blank for me. But he didn't go directly to his brother."

"Yeah, he told me about his schizophrenia, that he has trouble following through on things, that he got distracted easily, and that it took him a couple of days to remember what he was planning, and by then he was on to something else."

That explained why Joel had hung around Trenton for a few days, staying at the Rescue Mission and the old shul. But what finally motivated him to speak with Rob? And why had he been looking up temple elders on his brother's computer?

Chapter 14
Man of Honor

When I got home, I took a closer look at the members of the board of directors on the synagogue's website, but nothing jumped out at me. I knew all those people, some of them since I was a child, and it was hard to see them as an outsider would.

Eventually I gave up, heated up the leftover lasagna and sat at the kitchen table, surfing through the New Jersey state archives on my laptop. Though some microfilmed materials were available online, most of the material in the searchable databases dealt with the early history of the state. All I could find was general information and census data of the Jewish population in Trenton in the 1940s and 50s.

I spoke to Lili for a while, letting her vent, but I could tell that she was starting to figure out how she could fit into the equation down there, what she could do to help. "I wish I'd insisted that she get long-term care insurance," Lili said. "Back when she was young enough and healthy enough to qualify. She always insisted she had enough money to carry her through, but now that I look at the cost of rehab facilities and in-home nursing care, I'm not sure. At least Medicare will pay for what she needs now."

"Do you think we should have long term care insurance

ourselves?" I asked. "Health care power of attorney and all that? You and I don't have any no legal ties, so what if one of us were to get into an accident or get sick, and someone like Fedi comes in to take over? I don't even have any close enough family."

"*Dios mio*, Steve. Don't you think I have enough to take care of down here?"

"Sorry, sorry. I was just thinking."

She sighed. "I know, and you're right. Just let me get through this, all right?"

"Of course, sweetheart. You focus on your mother right now. Everything between us will work itself out. Everything all right in your office?"

"So far, so good. You're not taking Rochester over there tomorrow, are you?"

I usually left Rochester at Lili's office when I taught my Tuesday class. "No, I was thinking I'd take him to Rick's. He and Rascal can play together, and Rick has a guy who comes over to let Rascal out into the yard in the afternoon."

That night, Rochester slept beside me once again, and I woke up to see him sitting on his haunches staring at me. "What?" I grumbled. I looked over at the clock. It was barely seven in the morning.

He stepped over me and settled down on my chest. "Get off of me, you beast," I said, shoving at his side. "You're cutting off my circulation."

He just looked at me.

"Fine, I'm getting up." I pulled the comforter and over his body, tucking it around his head like a bonnet. "Little Gold Riding Hood."

He wriggled out from underneath and jumped to the floor, barking once. I stumbled to the bathroom then put on a pair of sweats and a long-sleeved T-shirt and we were out the door.

An hour later, we were at Rick's, and he yawned as he opened his front door. Rochester nearly bowled him over in his eagerness to get to Rascal. "Good morning to you, too," Rick said to the dog's departing behind.

"I thought you'd be up and on your way to work by now." "Usually would be. But I was out late last night, interviewing

people on the bus route that goes past the synagogue. No one I spoke to can remember anything from last Wednesday. Nobody noticed Joel, or the skinhead he had a beef with at the Rescue Mission. I'm still working on tracking the guy, though John White is not exactly a unique name."

I called Rochester to me and told him to be a good boy. I tried to pet him, but he skidded away again to play.

So much for doggie love.

Maybe it was Lili's absence, or not having Rochester with me, but I was glad to escape Friar Lake and drive the few miles to the Eastern campus for the Jewish American Lit class.

I was looking forward to some great discussion, and I wanted to introduce the ideas that I'd come up with while searching the immigration databases, but before I could get started, Jessica demanded, "Why aren't we reading Elie Wiesel's *Night*? Isn't the Holocaust important enough for this class?"

I was surprised by her hostility but I tried to diffuse it. "Weisel's book is a literary classic, and one that is deeply connected to the Jewish experience of the twentieth century," I said. "To answer your question, we can look at the title of this course—it's called Jewish-American literature, and the focus of the syllabus and our readings is to examine the experience of immigration and assimilation."

"But how can you look at the Jewish-American experience without considering the effect of the Holocaust?" she said. "A whole branch of my family was wiped out by the Nazis, and my great-grandparents had to struggle to escape. That has to color everything that my family, and by extension, American Jews, go through."

"I empathize with you," I said. "But I'll posit that perhaps that experience, while traumatic, means less to certain people. Remember, there have been Jews in America since before the Revolutionary War. And while their descendants may have been moved by the Holocaust, it isn't their primary narrative."

Noah jumped in. "It's like ancient history already," he said. "Yeah, my family lost people then, too. But they weren't people I knew. Like I'm going to get all stressed over my grandmother's second cousin? I'm more interested in how my grandfather couldn't go to the college he wanted to because they had a Jewish quota."

"Well, you're just selfish," Jessica said.

The class erupted in argument, and it took me several minutes to get them all calmed down. We ended up talking about different paths to citizenship, and I used Lili's family as an example of Jews who weren't able to gain admittance to the US due to restrictive immigration policies. "And isn't that something we see today?" I asked.

We did finally get into a good discussion—connected more to current events than the literature we'd been reading—but I figured any time I could get students thinking and talking I had done my job. Since I didn't have Rochester with me, I decided to go back to Trenton and look through the archives again, and see if I could figure out what Joel Goldberg had been looking for. Unfortunately, the librarian on duty at the New Jersey State Archives wasn't as helpful as Akiva Teitelboim. She couldn't remember anything about a homeless guy coming in to look up information on Jews in the city, but she directed me to a collection of microfilm called the Trenton Jewish History Project. I confess that I forgot all about Joel as I read about Jewtown, making connections to streets and family names from my childhood.

One article called it a closed community – the streets rang with the sound of Yiddish, and kosher butchers, stores, milk dealers, and a synagogue and a *mikveh* ritual bath provided everything that residents needed. Rents were inexpensive, and sidewalks, street lights and indoor plumbing eventually appeared. A trolley car ran down Broad Street, providing a connection to the rest of the city.

I relished the list of names of early residents – Lavine, Feinberg, Haveson, Silverstein, Levy, Kohn. Many of those reminded me of kids I'd gone to Hebrew school or Sunday school with, or people my mother had grown up with. This truly was my home, I thought.

But I wasn't at the archives for a stroll down memory lane. I was trying to figure out what Joel Goldberg was looking for. I moved more quickly through the microfilm, scanning for the names Aaron and Kalman.

I found a butcher named Kalman Horowitz with a store in Jewtown called Liberty Meat Market. Was he the Kalman of the postcard? Not if the photo had been taken in Europe around the time of World War II.

I found several albums of digitized photos that had been uploaded by community members. I didn't recognize much, because most had been taken in that area of Jewtown that had been destroyed by urban renewal. The people in the photos were all strangers, too, until I saw my mother's face, smiling from a photo of members of the Young Judea group for members in their late teens and early twenties, organized by Shomrei Torah.

It was surprisingly poignant to see her image when I wasn't expecting it. The occasion was a lecture by Kalman Feinberg, a Holocaust survivor. He had been lucky enough to avoid the camps, and spoke to the group about the years he had spent in hiding. Feinberg, a slim, dark-haired man in a business suit and black fedora, had then been given an award by the club's officers. My mother, Sylvia Gordon, was the club secretary. From the date on the picture, she was about sixteen.

Was he the Kalman I was looking for? He appeared to be in his mid to late thirties, so about the right age to match the boy in the photo. But I couldn't find any other references to him in the database.

I sat back in my chair. If he was the guy I was looking for, then he had a brother named Aaron Feinberg. Clearly his brother wasn't the current president of Shomrei Torah—he was much too young. But suppose Kalman's brother had died in the Holocaust? It made sense that he'd name his son after his late brother, in the Ashkenazi tradition.

But then I remembered something my mother had told me, long before, when we were visiting graves in the cemetery in Trenton where my grandparents were buried. I was probably about seven or eight at that time, and I had pointed out a gravestone in the shape of a tree trunk, cut off with a horizontal slice. "That one's pretty," I'd said. "When I die I want a tombstone like that one."

"Don't say that," my mother had said. She spit twice on the ground in a gesture that frightened me. She explained that stones like that were erected to memorialize children whose lives had been cut short. "And that's their only memorial. It's bad luck to name a baby after a child who died young, so their name is never carried on."

If Kalman Feinberg's brother had died young, then it was unlikely he'd have given his son the name. I still made a note of it.

I read as much as I could about the history of Shomrei Torah. The rabbi in the 1940s was named Jacob Sapinsky, and he was involved with the Hebrew Sheltering Home, which provided a refuge for Holocaust survivors. He had died in 1948 at the age of fifty. I found only one reference which indicated that he had been murdered; most of what I read were tributes to him as a man of honor.

Was his death connected to what Joel had found? Could Rabbi Sapinsky have been the one who secreted those documents behind the Belgian block wall? He was the rabbi of the congregation, and he had access to the area. But then, so could anyone else who belong to the shul at that time.

The question was why hide those papers? And what did they mean?

Chapter 15
Call Me Al

I needed to speak to Rick about what I'd found, so I called him as I left the library in Trenton. "How would you feel about me bringing over pizza when I come for Rochester?" I asked.

"That would be awesome. I'm just wrapping up here at work and I don't have the energy to fix anything."

Rick had just gotten home when I arrived with the pizza, and he quickly pulled out the last two Dogfish Head Firefly Ales from the six pack. The dogs circled around us as if they hadn't eaten in days, and as we ate we both fed them pieces of crust.

I told him about speaking with Akiva the librarian. "So that might explain what brought Joel to Trenton. But something sidetracked him and I think it has to do with the documents he found at the old shul." I munched a slice of pizza, the crust chewy, the toppings as gooey and delicious as I remembered. "You find anything interesting today?" I asked after a while.

"I did some research on the bus ticket in Joel Goldberg's pocket," Rick said. "I wanted to see if I could figure out where he'd been. I called a buddy of mine on the Trenton PD and he told me that the police stopped Joel in Hiltonia because he was making a racket and banging on the door of a house in the neighborhood. He told the officers some story about needing a way to get to the train station and so they took him to the station in West Trenton and dropped him there."

"That makes sense," I said. "He had looked up bus schedules at the library, so he knew there was a bus from the station that would take him to Shomrei Torah. Do you know the address where he was banging?"

"It was a neighbor who called, and by then Joel had moved down the street, so they don't have an exact address."

"But they have the neighbor's address, right? You could contact the neighbor and find out who was being harassed."

"I can get it from my buddy but it means calling in a favor."

"I do. You ever track down that skinhead that Buddha McCarthy mentioned?"

"Yeah. He ripped off a convenience store in West Trenton the day after he had his fight at the Rescue Mission. Been in jail ever since. And surprisingly enough, his name really is John White. At least that's what's on his ID."

By the time we were finished the dogs had eaten so much crust, and bits of sausage, that they weren't interested in kibble. We took them out for a long walk around Rick's neighborhood. Rochester was eager to investigate all the different smells and I kept having to tug him along to keep up with Rascal who was, as my father would have said, on a "mission: pishin'."

I took Rochester home soon after that, stopping at the mailboxes to pick up my mail. There was a letter from Daniel Epstein, and when I got home I opened it to find the original document I'd given him as well as his rough translation.

As he had said, it was a testimony from a Holocaust survivor named Myer Hafetz, about the fates of the people from his neighborhood in Berlin.

At last, I found the Aaron and Kalman I'd been looking for. They were brothers who had lived a few blocks from Hafetz. He described their childhood, how he and Kalman had celebrated their bar mitzvah the same year, 1938, right before the first round up of Jews.

As teenagers, he and Kalman, and Kalman's younger brother Aaron, had survived the increasing roundups that followed *Kristallnacht* when Jewish shops and synagogues were vandalized. They had tried to lay low, but in 1941, after Jews were forced to wear the yellow Star of David badges, they had been sent to Auschwitz. Aaron, who was a skinny youth, *oysgedart* in Yiddish, had been immediately sent to the gas chamber, while Kalman Feinberg was put to work at a nearby factory.

Hafetz had been assigned to the camp's kitchens, and his skill at creating the traditional German dishes he had learned from his mother kept him alive as he saw his old friend gradually decline. He tried to slip extra food to Kalman whenever he could but it was no use. Three months before the camp was liberated in 1945, thousands of internees were massacred by the camp's guards, including Kalman Feinberg and many others from Hafetz's neighborhood in Berlin. Hafetz only survived because he was needed to cook for the staff.

The sheer volume of names was chilling. Hafetz had brought to life his family, friends and neighbors, listing their approximate ages, their jobs, even physical details like red hair or a limp. I couldn't imagine the strength that had been required to survive Auschwitz, let alone recreate the experience, and the deaths of so many.

But how had that document, and the photo of the two boys, ended up at the old shul? I went back online to the immigration records and searched for Myer Hafetz. I discovered that he had spent two years after the liberation of Auschwitz in a camp for displaced persons and eventually been connected to a distant cousin in New York who had sponsored him to come to the United States.

There the trail disappeared. What had happened to Hafetz? And how did what he wrote connect to Joel's death?

Lili called later that evening. "Hallelujah," she said. "They released my mother to rehab this afternoon. A very nice facility not far from where Fedi and Sara live. Medicare will pay a hundred percent for the first three weeks."

"I'm delighted," I said.

"I'm going to stay at least another day, make sure she's settled, then I'll come home. Though I have to admit it's been nice here, aside from the problems with my mother. It's so warm and it's always sunny. And there's some kind of alchemy going on. Every time I walk into a store the clerks start speaking to me in Spanish. I like it."

I wasn't sure that I would appreciate someone addressing me in a foreign language in the United States, but then I didn't speak Spanish. We talked for a few more minutes, and I got up and walked around the living room as I told Lili what I'd discovered in the translation.

Rochester was agitated, and after I finished the call I sat on the sofa to pet him. He swished his big tail a couple of times and a bunch of papers flew off the coffee table. One of them was the Septa bus schedule I'd picked up at the library in Trenton.

Joel Goldberg had ridden that bus just one week earlier. Rick had interviewed the driver and the passengers he'd been able to find. But what if someone only rode the bus on Tuesday nights? I knew lots of people whose routine deviated one or two nights a week, due to classes, clubs, or some other obligation.

I looked at the clock. If I left in the next half hour, I could make it to the West Trenton railroad station in time to pick up the same bus Joel had taken. Was it worth the trouble, since Rick had already determined there were no leads there?

Why not? Rochester had given me the clue, right? It was up to me to follow it.

I was startled when my cell phone rang as I was about to leave the house with the distinctive ringtone I'd assigned to Rick. Did he know what I was about to do? I doubted he'd approve.

But instead all he wanted to do was tell me that he had called the neighbor who'd reported seeing Joel Goldberg in Hiltonia the week before, but had to leave a voice mail message.

We chatted for a minute or two then I ended the call and hurried out to my car. Rochester wasn't happy to be left behind, but I doubted Septa would appreciate his presence on the bus.

I boarded the bus while it idled in the station waiting for the train to arrive. I spoke briefly to the driver, who said he'd been off the night that Joel was killed, as Rick had discovered. I went over to the other half-dozen people on the bus, and none of them remembered anything unusual about the previous Thursday.

The train pulled in and a guy in his twenties jumped off and hurried over to board the bus, a messenger bag slung over his shoulder. Before I could get up and speak to him, the bus pulled out, and I was on for the ride.

I watched him for moment to feel out how to approach him, and while I did, he put his phone to his head and pulled a thick textbook from his bag. I realized he was going over material with someone on the other end, and he would probably shut me right down if I interrupted him.

I'd have to wait until he hung up, or got off the bus, to speak with him. The bus moved onward through the darkness, the way forward lit only by the glow of its headlights, and the guy stayed on the phone.

I pulled out the schedule, hoping that the bus was on a continuous loop, and that if I stayed on long enough, I'd be able to get back off at the train station on the next run.

Oops. This was the last run of the night. The last stop was on the road to New Hope, a couple of miles north of Stewart's Crossing. It was going to be a long walk home.

As we pulled up to the stop beside Shomrei Torah, the young guy ended his call and closed his textbook. He jumped up, and I followed him off the bus. At least I was a lot closer to home there.

"Excuse me," I said. "I wonder if I could ask you a couple of questions."

He looked suspicious as the bus pulled out. He was a couple of inches shorter than I was, and about twenty years younger. He wore khaki pants and a polo shirt with a lanyard around his neck holding an ID card. There was something Asian about his face but I couldn't place where he might have been from.

"My name is Steve Levitan, and I'm helping a friend out. His brother was on this bus last Thursday—a guy in his late twenties, might have looked homeless. Do you remember him? His name was Joel Goldberg."

He picked up on the past tense right away. "I remember him. He was carrying an old backpack. You said was?"

I nodded. "He was killed that night, here on the grounds of the synagogue. He was the rabbi's brother."

His mouth opened, and he swallowed hard. "Wow. I've never known anyone who was killed. I mean, not that I knew him, but we talked for a minute when we got off the bus. He had this stone in his hand, a really pretty green one, and I asked him about it."

He shook his head. "I need to sit down."

He sat on the bus bench and after a moment I joined him there. "I'm Albert Paca," he said. "You can call me Al." He swallowed again.

I nodded along. "You live somewhere nearby?"

"Just on the other side of the hill. I work in Philly and I usually drive back and forth, but on Tuesday evenings I have a class at Temple."

I wasn't sure if he laughed or hiccupped, and then he said, "Not a temple like this one. The university."

"You look pretty tired. I'm not surprised you wouldn't want to drive. I won't keep you for long, I promise. What did he say when you spoke to him?"

"Just that he always carried the stone with him because it made him feel calmer. He kept rubbing his thumb over it, like he was really worried about something."

The malachite worry stone Rochester had found in the grass. Further evidence that the man Al had spoken to was Joel Goldberg.

"I figured he was there to meet someone," Al said. "Because as I was walking home a car passed me, going fast, and zoomed into the parking lot."

Had that been Joel's killer, arriving to meet him? "Did you notice anything about the car?"

He shook his head. "Just that it was going too fast for these dark roads."

Al Paca had nothing more to add. He stuffed his thick textbook into his messenger bag and stood up. "I hope they find whoever killed him," he said. "Even homeless people are human beings."

"They are," I said. I watched him walk away, and then called Rick. "Do me a favor? Come pick me up at Shomrei Torah?"

"What are you doing there at this time of night?"

"I met a guy who rode the bus with Joel Goldberg the night he was killed."

Rick let out a big sigh. "Hold that thought. I'll be there in fifteen."

While I waited I walked up to the shul. Motion-sensor lights on the outside lit up, but I was able to stay in the shadows. I wondered if there were any security alarms on the property that might have been activated—but if there had been, then someone would have discovered Joel's body earlier, and Rick or the rabbi would certainly have mentioned them.

I tried to put myself back in the scene. Joel had gotten off the bus and begun walking toward the shul. Then the car Al Paca had seen had pulled into the parking lot.

Was Joel expecting him? Or was the person in the car following him? How could he or she have known where Joel was going?

Rick's headlights swiped across the parking lot as he pulled in, and I walked over to his truck and climbed in. "How did you meet someone when I couldn't?" he demanded.

I shrugged. "I had this idea that maybe someone only rode the bus one day a week." I explained what I had heard from Al Paca, about his Tuesday night class, his encounter with Joel, the fast-moving car that had pulled into the parking lot. "He said Joel had his backpack with him that night, but you never found it, did you? Wouldn't that imply that the killer took the backpack?"

"Imply is the right word."

By the time we got to the railroad station, Rick was mollified.

"Give me the guy's full name," he said, and he wrote it down. "I'll call him tomorrow and verify what you told me."

"I'm not trying to take over your job, you know," I said. "I just had this hunch and I didn't want to bother you with it."

"And the dog was involved somehow, wasn't he?" "He knocked the bus schedule off the coffee table."

Rick shook his head. "You and the dog. You and the dog."

Chapter 16
First Fruits

Rochester and I both overslept the next morning, and it was a scramble to get him fed and walked, scarf down some breakfast myself, and head to Shomrei Torah for my second week of Bible study. I also wanted to thank Daniel Epstein for helping with the Yiddish translation.

Rabbi Goldberg had already started when Rochester and I arrived, though, so I slid into a chair beside Daniel with a quick apology. Rochester moved over to sniff Sadie and then slump down beside her. "Welcome," Rabbi said. "We've just begun discussing this week's *parasha*, a Torah reading called *Ki Tavo*. What God is telling us here is basically not to procrastinate, not to put off obeying God's commandments, because we're never going to have that stress-free day with no other responsibilities. We must utilize all our days to the maximum."

He sighed. "This parasha has special meaning to me, because of the recent death of my brother Joel. Did I spend time every day showing him that I loved him? No. Did I do my best to help him through his illness? I have to admit that I did not. There were always other pressures, from life, other family, members of the congregation. What God is telling us here is to realize those obligations, both to the great spirit and to those around us, and not procrastinate in fulfilling them."

I thought of Lili, in Florida with her mother. She had delayed in dealing with Senora Weinstock's illness, and this was the result—an emergency visit to try and patch things up. That wasn't good for either of them, or her brother and sister-in-law.

What could she do, though, from Pennsylvania? There was only so much one could accomplish in a phone call. I knew that, from my regulated calls to my father from prison as he was in his last days. I had felt terrible about my inability to be there with him, blaming the California penal system rather than accepting the responsibility for my own actions. Since then I'd come to peace with the situation – my father knew that I loved him. He had someone to take care of him, and he didn't linger in pain waiting for me to come to him.

I was startled out of my reverie when Rochester came over to sniff my hand. I petted him and he settled beside me.

"This parasha also mentions *bikkurim*, the first fruits," the rabbi continued. "That it is our obligation to take our first ripened fruits to the Temple. But this is not a tithe, or a requirement to feed the priests. Instead, it's a way to remind us that we are not the Creator, that all we have is a gift from God. Everything from the fruits of the vine to our loved ones."

We talked for a while, and then the rabbi wished us Shalom, and everyone stood up to leave. I walked over to him and asked, "Do you know where in Europe your family came from?"

"Back then, it was all Russia," he said. "My father's parents came from Lithuania, and my mother's father from Belarus. Not sure about my mother's mother—we could never find a town by the name she mentioned on the map."

"But not Berlin? Or Germany?" He shook his head. "Why?"

"Just something I'm working on."

The rabbi lowered his voice. "I'm worried. Aaron Feinberg has been pressing me for details about what the police know about Joel's death. He has been cloaking it with the idea that he's protecting the congregation, but I'm worried that he may be collecting evidence to get me removed as rabbi. Just like what happened in Milwaukee."

So the rabbi was worried about losing his job. Worried enough to have killed his brother to protect it? But then why ask me to snoop into Joel's whereabouts and actions?

And why was Feinberg so interested in Joel's death? Did he know more about what had gone on that evening than he was letting on?

"I was able to figure out Joel's email password," the rabbi continued. "I started looking through what he'd been reading and writing. He seemed to be focused on something that had happened during the Holocaust that still had reverberations today. But it was too upsetting for me to read."

He looked at me. "You have a computer background, don't you? If I gave you the password, could you look through my brother's email account and see if there's anything there that might tell me what he wanted from me?"

A tiny jolt of electricity buzzed through my brain. Offered access to someone's private email? A password into someplace online I didn't belong? That was just what had gotten me into trouble in the past. But because I was doing it on the rabbi's behalf, it wouldn't be illegal.

But I might be able to help the rabbi, and maybe even help Rick bring Joel Goldberg's killer to justice. Of course I had to say yes.

I gave the rabbi my email address, thanked him and wished him shalom, and then put Rochester's leash on and hurried out to catch up with Daniel Epstein. He was leaning heavily on his cane, his shoulders hunched, and his face looked grayer and more lined than it had only a few days before when I'd seen him at his home.

"Thanks for the translation," I said. "It's very interesting."

"You're welcome. It was a challenge to figure out some of the Yiddish."

Aaron Feinberg joined us then, wearing a dark suit, crisp white shirt and blood-red tie. "You're a translator now?" he asked Epstein. "*Ir leyenen Yiddish?*"

"I can read it, but not as well as I wish," Daniel said. "Mostly I grew up speaking it with my parents. How about you?"

"My father spoke German but not Yiddish," Feinberg said. "He was raised in a secular family. But I learned a little from listening to my mother and her family. Can't read any of it, though."

"Steve found a document in Yiddish he needed help understanding. A Holocaust survivor's story."

Feinberg turned to me. "Why would you care about such a thing? That's old news to someone your age."

So much for the "never forget" mantra that had been drilled into us in Sunday school. "I hope the Holocaust is still important for generations to come," I said, a bit icily.

Feinberg humphed and stalked away. "I think you offended our esteemed president," Epstein said with a smile. "He's getting more and more touchy lately." He leaned close. "I think he's worried someone younger will challenge him for synagogue presidency."

"Well, I believe what I said. George Santayana said those who forget history are doomed to repeat it, and I'd rather not get rounded up and placed in an internment camp or a gas chamber."

"I agree with that. I heard too many stories of the camps when I was a child."

"I've been thinking about that paper and how it might have ended up behind the wall at the old shul. Did you ever worship there?"

"Oh, yes, it's where I celebrated my bar mitzvah. The rabbi then reminds me a lot of our Rabbi Goldberg. Young and enthusiastic. What a terrible shame he was dead only a few years later."

"I read about his death when I was doing some research online, but I couldn't find any information. Do you know what happened to him?"

"I don't remember the details, but I know no one ever found out who killed him. It was a real tragedy, that. I collected all the newspaper articles about his death, if you want to know more."

"I'd appreciate that. I'm not sure what I'm looking for but I feel like something happened back in the 1940s that might have some reverberations today."

"I'm going home now. Would you like to stop by? Or do you have to be at work?"

"I'm my own boss," I said, which was technically true, though I did report to the college president. "If you don't mind that I bring Rochester with me, I can come by now."

Epstein reached down to scratch Rochester's head with the hand that wasn't balanced on the cane. "A sweet dog like you is always welcome at my house," he said.

I took Rochester over to the woods beside the sanctuary for a sniff and a pee, and by the time we got back to my car and drove to Epstein's house, he was just pulling his battered Toyota sedan into his garage.

"Everything is in my office, the second bedroom on the right," Epstein said as he ushered us inside. He stopped to scratch behind Rochester's ears, and the dog gave him a goofy grin. "Most of the documents from back then are organized by years, piled on the shelves. You'll forgive me if I don't lead you up there."

"I'll be fine." I started up the stairs as Rochester followed Epstein into the living room. I knew that my dog would be well-taken care of while I immersed myself in whatever Epstein had collected.

The second bedroom had a desk, an ergonomic chair, and built in cabinets along the walls. The desk was piled with papers, and there were shopping bags full of more paper in a neat row along one wall.

I began sorting through Epstein's folders to find the material from the time after the Second World War. I felt like an archaeologist sifting through layers of history.

I sat on the floor with a teetering stack of newspapers, magazines and manila folders and began to go through them. I heard Epstein talking to Rochester, and the click of doggie toenails on a wooden floor somewhere, and then I was quickly lost in the 1940s.

Daniel had been born in 1932, and graduated from Trenton High in 1948. I found the program from his graduation and scanned through the names, some of them the same as those I'd found in the archives of Jewtown.

He had saved an article from the Trenton *Times* about the graduating class, and he was one of the few who was headed to college—New Jersey State Teachers College at Trenton, in his case. That was the predecessor to Trenton State, which had eventually become the College of New Jersey.

Rochester came into the room and sniffed at the pile beside me. I reached out to pet him as I flipped through a lot of stuff from Epstein's college years—old football programs, dance cards, papers he'd written and tests he'd taken. Man, this guy hadn't thrown anything away, had he?

Rochester lifted his paw and pushed the pile of material over, scattering everything on the tongue-and-groove flooring. "Oh, crap," I said. He had his nose down on one particular folder, and when I picked it up I found that Epstein had labeled it "Rabbi Sapinsky."

"Good boy," I said to Rochester, even though it was going to be a pain to clean up all the paperwork. "This is just what I was looking for."

He slumped down on the floor beside me, his back resting against my thigh, and I began to read. The first papers were programs from High Holy Day services at the old shul, where he'd been asked to read from the Torah one Yom Kippur. Beneath those was a series of articles from the *Trentonian*, the old morning paper, and the *Trenton Evening Times*.

We'd gotten both papers delivered when I was a kid, the *Trentonian* a tabloid that came before breakfast, while the Trenton *Times* showed up in the afternoon.

The first mention of Rabbi Sapinsky came on a March day in the *Times*. The headline of the short article was "Rabbi Found Dead in Jewtown."

The body of Rabbi Jacob Sapinsky, 50, was found in the sanctuary of his synagogue, Shomrei Torah on New Street, late yesterday evening. The rabbi was not known to be in poor health, though according to a police source he had been very involved with the Hebrew Sheltering Home. This facility, which has brought many Eastern European immigrants to Trenton, has been cited as a hotbed of contagious diseases including lung disease, influenza and tuberculosis.

The paper didn't mention whether the rabbi had died of natural causes or something more violent, just inferred that because he had helped immigrants he might have caught something from one of them. It was the kind of xenophobic attitude I expected from certain right-wing publications even today.

The next morning's article, from the *Trentontian*, was much more inflammatory, with a big headline that read "Second Murder in Jewtown."

According to the writer, the police had revealed further details of the rabbi's death; he had been shot at close range, his body discovered at the shul an hour after the end of the evening service.

The article went on to imply that crime was rising in Trenton because of an influx of Jews and other refugees from Eastern Europe. This was the second homicide in six months in Jewtown, the reporter noted, and he believed that the rabbi's murder was a symptom of discord between established residents and new immigrants.

A second murder, before Rabbi Sapinsky? Who was the victim?

There was nothing in Epstein's archive about that earlier crime.

There were a few more articles on the rabbi's death, but no new details were revealed, and it appeared that no one was ever charged. Beneath the articles was a single sheet of paper that reminded me of the mimeographed newsletters that were common when I was a kid, before everyone had access to copying machines. This one was headlined "To the members of Shomrei Torah," and the blue printing was fuzzy and fading. At least it was written in English so I didn't need anyone to translate it for me.

"Our rabbi's death was a tragedy," I read. "But members of

Shomrei Torah are cautioned to avoid agitating with regard to the cause of his death. The Jewish position in the United States is still tenuous, and as a minority it is in our best interest to retain a low profile. Calls for further investigation by the police can only cause our community to be in the spotlight in a negative manner."

The message was unsigned, and I wondered if it had come from an individual member or from the office of the shul.

When I was young, my grandmother and my great-aunts viewed everything that happened through the lens of "is it good for the Jews?" When a Jewish actor or musician won an award, they kvelled. When a Jew was arrested for theft or accused of some other crime, they agonized over the larger implications for us and our people.

Statistics I had found noted that the Jewish population of Trenton during that time comprised about six percent of the total. Was this is a case of fear of xenophobia? Or was someone trying to cover up the rabbi's murder?

I went downstairs with a pile of material I wanted to take a closer look at. Daniel Epstein was dozing in an easy chair, but he woke at the sound of my footsteps on the wood floor. The poor guy looked ancient, and I hoped that he'd be able to get back to sleep after Rochester and I left.

"Do you mind if I borrow this material? I'll bring it all back when I'm done."

"Have you found something interesting?" He sat up in his chair and pulled on his glasses, and he looked a decade younger, and more vibrant.

"I read the articles you saved from the newspaper. But there was never any mention of a solution to the rabbi's murder."

"It was a shonda, *that*," he said, using the Yiddish word for a sin. "People in the Jewish community wanted the murders hushed up because they were afraid the goyim would rise up against us if they thought we were criminals."

"You said murders," I said, remembering the brief note I'd read about a second death in Jewtown before the Rabbi's. "There was another?"

"A cousin of the Namias family, I believe. At least, he stayed with them for a while. He worked at the junkyard they owned on New Street."

"Do you know what happened to him?"

"He was found dead in an alley beside the junkyard. But Henry would know more."

"Henry Namias? From the rabbi's Talmud study group?"

"That's the one. You should talk to him. I'll call him if you want, introduce you."

I said that would be great, and he made the call. "Henry, it's Daniel Epstein," he said. Then he looked confused. He looked up at me. "Awful things, these answering machines and voice mail. I never know if I'm talking to a person or a machine." Then he turned back to the phone and left a message for Henry to call him.

Daniel already had my phone number, and he promised to call me once he'd spoken to Namias. "He's an *alter kocker*, that one," he said, using the name for a cranky old man. "But don't you worry, I'll soften him up for you."

By then, Rochester had his head in Epstein's lap. "As if anybody needs to be softened up for you, you sweet boy," he said, scratching behind Rochester's ears.

I had long ago accepted that people often liked my dog better than they did me. I hoped that might be the case with Henry Namias, too.

I wasn't sure at all what I was looking for, but it seemed that the more I dug, the more unsolved murders in the past I came up with. Had Joel figured something out about those crimes? There was no statute of limitations on murder, but it was doubtful that whoever had killed Rabbi Sapinsky, and Henry Namias's cousin, was still alive and able to have killed Joel. I'd have to look back at the time line to be sure, though.

Chapter 17
Relevant Information

It was nearly noon by the time we left Daniel Epstein's house, and I drove too quickly up the twisting, turning River Road to Friar Lake because I felt guilty about taking so long away on a work day. I swerved to avoid a family of ducks crossing the road on their way to the river, a big brown Muscovy hen leading a parade of chicks behind her.

Rochester sat up and woofed at them but the ducks were focused on their mission. I had a commitment, too, to my job, and if I didn't pay attention to it, everything I had built over the past two years might be torn apart.

Before I began working at Eastern, I had only an ordinary sense of alumni affection for the college. I had spent four years there, learned how to apply my brain to problems, fallen in and out of love, made friends and gathered mentors. But then I'd moved on, first to Columbia, where I got my master's, and then to California, where my dreams of creating a family of my own bit the dust.

The community at Eastern had become a second family to me over the last two years. I'd made friends on the faculty and staff, attended events, bonded with students. Though I was working off campus, I still felt connected to those old buildings at the top of the hill in Leighville and the way that a college education can shape a life. I felt very lucky to be part of that community, to be able to give back in return for so much that had been given to me.

I carried Epstein's box into the office with me and left it on the coffee table in the reception area of the gatehouse, beside the pile of brochures advertising Friar Lake's conference facilities.

Fortunately, nothing had happened in my absence other than the receipt of a flood of emails in my inbox. I ate the sandwich I'd made for lunch as I skipped through them, deleting the irrelevant ones and reading the ones I had to. Professor Del Presto had sent me a draft of her ideas for an immigration program, focused on the way that hashtags like #shutthedoor and #immigrationreform had their roots in historical attitudes of isolationism.

I was reminded of that bumper sticker in the shape of the continental U.S., and the belief it represented that we ought to close the door to outsiders. What if my own grandparents hadn't been able to enter the U.S. when they left Russia and Lithuania? Would I have been born in Cuba like Lili, in Argentina like Akiva the librarian? What about all the accomplishments of immigrants, and those descended from immigrants?

Those thoughts reminded me I had to check the college's learning management system to see if my students in the Jewish American Lit class had sent me any messages of made any new discussion posts.

With Rochester sprawled on the floor beside me, I began to read and grade posts. I loved the way students came up with oddball ideas that had never occurred to me, took the work in different directions or went off on tangents.

Jessica, the girl who looked like an extra in *Fiddler*, had written that she was interested in the ways that the authors we were reading had reinterpreted Bible stories to fit their lives. "So far I've recognized allusions to Adam and Eve, Cain and Abel, and King David and the way he stole Bathsheba from Uriah," she wrote.

Interesting that she'd found references to three different stories that revolved around family—the very first family, according to the

Bible, and the way it, and the marriage of Uriah and Bathsheba, had fallen apart.

I wished she'd been more specific—which work had referenced which story? I responded to her comment congratulating her on her insight and asking for more details. Other students had shared their observations about the insularity of immigrant communities, that perhaps when they stayed so close together they prevented assimilation and that might lead to prejudice against them.

Noah, the student whose family came from Trenton, had written, "If you focus only on your family and not your neighbors, who can blame those people from suspecting you? We're always frightened of what we don't know."

I wrote back that at least in Kaplan's book immigrants from various countries all bonded together in common pursuit of English fluency, and that perhaps that kind of joint effort would lead to more understanding.

When I finished, I looked around for Rochester. He'd gotten up and left my side, and taken up a position by the coffee table, beside where I'd left Epstein's box. Did he remember the smell of the man who'd been nice to him? Or was there was a clue in the box he wanted me to find?

I sat on the floor with the box on one side of me and Rochester on the other. I picked a folder at random and began flipping through it, until I stopped suddenly at the mention of my mother's name at the top of a form—and right beside hers was the name Victor Namias.

Every now and then I'd be surprised at the realization that my parents had lives before I was born. Letters my father had written home when he was in the Navy. A photo of my mother as a young woman, like the one I'd discovered online. And now this file.

In 1964, Shomrei Torah had launched an oral history project. Young volunteers were dispatched to synagogue members to ask them questions about old Trenton, about their younger years, and if they'd come from Europe, how they'd arrived in central New Jersey.

As I'd seen in that earlier picture, my mother was a member of the Young Judea Group at Shomrei Torah, and she'd volunteered, or been dragooned, into helping with the interviews. The document I'd found was a transcription of her conversation with a man named Victor Namias, who I eventually figured out was Henry's father.

It didn't seem like a coincidence to me – after all, the Jewish community in Trenton was relatively small, and I still knew a few of the people my mother had known when she was younger. If she was still alive, would she be able to fill in some of these blanks?

As I read through the document I recognized some of the same facts I'd found at the Jewtown blog.

My people come from Salonica. It was Turkey when they lived there, but now it's Greece. They call it Thessaloniki, but it's the same place. What can you do, the borders change all the time. In 1917 there was a big fire, fifty thousand people burned out of their homes. My parents decided it was time to leave and they came to America.

My family was Sephardic, from Spain long ago, and they spoke Ladino. I didn't even speak English until I went to school for the first time. We lived in this town outside New Brunswick, Highland Park. Lots of Sephardim there, we had our own shul, our own community. We looked after each other.

When I finished high school a friend of my father's from the shul got me a job with the same company he worked with, delivering baked goods. The only route they had was in Trenton, so I used to get up before the sun and drive the truck to the warehouse, load up the goods and then take them to stores around the city.

I met this beautiful girl, dark hair and dark eyes, named Esther, after the queen from the Bible. She worked at one of the stores down by the river in Jewtown, and I courted her for a while. She was only in this country a few years and she spoke mostly Yiddish but I taught her enough English that we could talk, and I could ask her to marry me.

I moved down to Trenton for good then, so she could be by her family and I didn't have so far to drive. Then her cousin got me a job in his junkyard, and eventually I became a partner. My wife would get pregnant and then lose the baby. Three times this happened, until finally our Henry was born. I said basta *then, enough, because I was afraid if we tried again I would lose my Esther, too.*

Esther is a real balabusta, *they call her in Yiddish, a good wife and a good woman. My queen. She's always taking in stray relatives. After the war we had one cousin after another staying with us until they could get their feet under them. Terrible things those people went through, worse than even my parents, losing everything in the great fire.*

The narrative continued for another page, but I stopped paying attention, thinking of my mother, twenty-two years old, listening to these stories. She was still living with her parents, working as a bookkeeper for a furniture store in Jewtown owned by neighbors. She had certainly known of the camps, and I knew that she'd lost some distant cousins, so surely the Holocaust had loomed in her consciousness.

Not for the first time, I missed my parents. I wished I could sit down with my mother and hear her talk more about what it had been like for her, growing up in Trenton after World War II.

Had she known Myer Hafetz, too? I did some quick calculations and realized she'd been a child when Hafetz died, so it was unlikely. But my grandparents probably knew the Namiases, and through them Hafetz.

It was curious how my own family history kept popping up in this investigation. What else would I discover—and would it be something I wished I hadn't?

I thought it would be a good idea to learn what I could about Henry Namias before I spoke with him, so I did some searching online for him.

He had no profiles on social media, though I found one of his grandchildren had mentioned him in a Facebook post. His family had donated an exercise room at Greenwood House, the Jewish home for the aged, and I found a few mentions of that gift. When I searched for "Namias" and "junkyard" I found an article on a blog dedicated to old Trenton.

> *The Namias family owned a junkyard on New Street in the heart of Jewtown. Victor Namias was from Turkey and spoke no Yiddish, so he focused on collecting used goods, cleaning them up and repairing them and his wife Esther, from Germany, spoke with customers and handled the books. Esther often took in refugees from the Hebrew Sheltering Home and there were always lively conversations going on in the office.*

Interesting. That matched what Daniel Epstein told me, that Myer Hafetz had been taken in by the Namias family when he came to Trenton. The mention of the Hebrew Sheltering Home echoed what Rick and I had found in the police files on Hafetz's death.

I sat back and thought about all that I'd discovered with relation to Joel Goldberg's death. It all seemed to circle back to the Holocaust.

Joel had found the photograph of those two boys at the old shul. Had he also found the testimony by Myer Hafetz and recognized the Hebrew characters that formed Yad Vashem? Maybe there was an English translation there, too, which Joel had taken away, leaving behind the one that he couldn't read.

If he had been able to read a translation, that might have refueled his obsession with the Holocaust and his need to speak with his brother, bringing him to Shomrei Torah on the Sunday morning of the Blessing of the Animals.

Why hadn't he brought the document to his brother, if he had seen it? He had the photo of the two boys folded up in his shoe. Did his killer take away the English translation?

These were all just theories, though. Since Joel's brain was affected by his schizophrenia, there was no way to know what he'd found or thought.

Something had driven him away from Shomrei Torah that Sunday, before he had a chance to speak to his brother. What was it?

Dog Is in the Details

The rabbi thought Joel had been using his computer, reviewing the members of the temple's board of directors. Because he was angry that Feinberg and his cabal had tried to chase him away?

As Buddha McCarthy had mentioned, Joel had a hard time following through on things because he'd get distracted. I knew one of the symptoms of schizophrenia was paranoia, though I didn't know if Joel suffered from that. It was reasonable, however, that he'd gotten sidetracked, thinking someone at the temple was out to get him.

Then something had happened over the next couple of days. Where was he living? He hadn't gone back to the Rescue Mission after his altercation with John White. Had he returned to the old shul? He had a backpack with him when he showed up on Sunday. Where was it? Had Rick found it on the temple grounds? I hadn't seen anything like it at the old shul when I went to investigate, and found the testimony from Myer Hafetz.

I called Rick and asked. "Nope, haven't found it," Rick said. "The rabbi mentioned it, too."

"Do you think whoever killed Joel took the backpack?" I asked. "Reasonable guess, since it was a remote area and the rabbi said his brother carried the pack with him everywhere. If we ever come up with a suspect I'll get a search warrant, but right now I'm low on clues and don't know where else to go. This is looking more and more like one for the cold case files."

I hung up, and since Rochester was restless, I took him out for a walk. Where could Joel's backpack be? What could he have been carrying that his killer might have wanted to take away? An English translation of the Yad Vashem document? More evidence that related to the boys in the photograph? Or something else entirely? Joel had been looking up the synagogue leadership at his brother's computer before he ran off—did he have something with him that connected to one of them?

I could see why Rick was baffled. I was, too. But I kept feeling that everything circled back to something that had happened in Trenton after the Holocaust. There were those two unsolved murders, after all. The Trentonian article I read mentioned only that Rabbi Sapinsky was the second victim. Who was the first?

I remembered what Rick had said about cold cases. Was it possible that there were records in Trenton of unsolved murders? Would they have been digitized?

As soon as Rochester and I got back to my office I started searching, and after a couple of false starts I found an article from the Trenton *Times* a couple of years before. The popularity of TV programs chasing down old homicides had led to pressure for a cold case squad to be formed in the Trenton Police Department, and old records dating back to the 1920s were being digitized.

My fingers tingled. Had the case file on the rabbi's murder been among those digitized? How could I find out? My first instinct was to wonder how good the security measures were around that data—could I hack into the database, with the tools I had?

Rochester nosed me then, and I realized I was standing at the top of a slippery slope. Hack into a police database? That was a sure road back to prison.

Time to shut down the computer and head home. I locked up my office, raced Rochester to the car, and settled down for the drive along River Road. I had downloaded an app from my insurance company that tracked my driving performance and could result in a lower rate, which meant I had to keep Bluetooth enabled on my cell phone so the app could communicate with a little gadget under my dash. I'd discovered I could play music from my phone through the car's speakers that way, too, and Rochester and I were enjoying a little Springsteen, the windows open and the music blasting.

I was startled as Bruce's voice was interrupted right in the middle of "My Hometown" by the theme from *Hawaii Five-O*.

It took me a moment to realize the car was channeling incoming calls, and then another to figure out how to accept the call. "Hello?" I asked a couple of times, before Rick responded.

"The ME has established that Joel Goldberg died sometime

between eleven PM, when Mr. Paca saw him get off the bus, and one AM."

"Does that mean that the person in the car Al Paca saw was Joel's killer?"

"It's a hypothesis," Rick said. "But right now there's nothing more than coincidence, so I'm not jumping to any conclusions. Paca didn't notice anything about the car, and without a description or a license plate there's no way to track it."

"But it is a piece of the puzzle." "That it is."

I told him about going to Daniel Epstein's house and the files he'd kept on the death of Rabbi Sapinsky, and what the document Epstein had translated had contained. "Can you ask your friend at the Trenton PD if the file on Rabbi Sapinsky's murder was digitized?"

"This is all irrelevant, you know," Rick said. "I'm trying to solve a murder that happened last week, not sixty years ago."

"I think it is relevant," I said. "I think Joel found something that ties to those old murders. And that information got him killed."

"I'll give it a try but I'm not making any promises," Rick said.

He ended the call and it took the Bluetooth a moment to recognize that, so suddenly my car was telling me that if I wanted to make a call I had to hang up and try again.

"Irrelevant information," I said to the disembodied voice.

Chapter 18
Unusual Agency

Lili called as I was fixing dinner. "I got a direct flight tomorrow that gets into Philadelphia at 3:30. Can you pick me up or should I take the train from the airport, and then connect to the one to Yardley?"

"Things are slow at Friar Lake, so I can pick you up. Text me your flight information. How's your mom doing in rehab?"

"Surprise, surprise, she likes it. She has a roommate, which I thought she'd hate, but she has someone to complain with about the food, the temperature, the therapists. The roommate doesn't speak a word of Spanish, which my mother would hate, too, but she loves, because she can say whatever she wants to me or Fedi and the woman doesn't understand."

"She's probably lonely," I said. "Living by herself. It will be good for her to socialize."

We talked for a few more minutes and then hung up. When I checked my email, I found that the rabbi had sent me his brother's address and password. I hoped that maybe there'd be a message there that would connect to what I'd previously found online, something that would give me an idea of what it was Joel was looking for.

Joel's email account was chock full of sent and received messages, many of them having to do with the Holocaust. He had emailed back and forth with a number of individuals he had met in forums online, often mentioning that it might be a while before he got back to them because he had to rely on public internet access. He had found someone whose family had emigrated to Trenton after leaving a camp, and he was trying to get that person to open up about his family background and what he knew, but the person was very cagey, always asking Joel more questions and never revealing too much.

Joel seemed obsessed, but I had to admit that I could be that way myself, particularly when it came to following a trail of evidence or justifying my need to hack into some protected spot online.

I was quickly overwhelmed by the emotion Joel's messages represented. Though his sentences were long and often wandered from topic to topic, the passion he felt was clear. No wonder Rabbi Goldberg hadn't been able to get through too many of the messages. I didn't have the same connection to Joel that the rabbi did, and even I couldn't read for more than an hour before I had to stop. Joel's passion and his intelligence were evident in his interactions, and it was painful to think of all that cut short.

I played tug-a-rope with Rochester for a while, then went out for a long walk around River Bend with him. When we got back, I sat down for a longer look at Joel Goldberg's email account. I needed to be organized if I was going to learn anything from this mass of data, so I created a spreadsheet to track it all. All those years in business had trained me to put information into columns and rows, looking for connections between bits and bytes.

I listed the email addresses, and where I had them, the real names of the people Joel had corresponded with. I created columns for people who were descendants of survivors, and others who were tracking family trees, and a third for people who were just curious, like a high school kid who went under the handle JohnnyBeBad, whom Joel had helped with a class report.

One of the problems I'd found in teaching at Eastern was that students weren't able to make judgments about which sources were most valid. I tried to teach them to look for credentials—was the person they were quoting an expert in the field? Did he or she have a degree or a job with a publication?

Too often they took what they found online as the gospel truth, often with bad consequences for their own work. One of my favorite examples was a student who'd written a paper about the Vietnam conflict, and his only source was a website called Marxism.org. Even though I tried to explain that this group represented the ideology on the losing side of the war, he never understood why their work could be biased.

I wondered what Johnny's teacher would say if Johnny revealed that his source was a homeless schizophrenic with no more than a high school education. Perhaps that wasn't quite fair to Joel – according to his brother, Joel was very intelligent, and the material he'd provided to Johnny was based on his own empirical research. But still – if I were the teacher I'd prefer a more credible source.

The only one of Joel's correspondents who really intrigued me was a man who went by the clunky handle of Not Who I Think I Am

– though with all the words jammed together without capitalization. He had grown up in Trenton, the son of a Holocaust survivor, and he was interested in learning anything he could about Auschwitz, particularly during the years 1943-45. His family had come from Berlin and he sought anyone who might have known an inmate named Karl Kurtz.

Joel had apparently done some research on the man's behalf, because he wrote that he had checked the archives in Trenton and been unable to find any record of Kurtz. He did include a note that mentioned the name was both German and Ashkenazi Jewish, derived from the German word for short. He had asked NotWho if he was a short man, but NotWho had not responded.

Reading Joel's emails about the after-effects of the Holocaust was fascinating, and I wanted to know more about what was going on in Trenton at that time. Were lots of survivors showing up? Was

Shomrei Torah a place that they congregated? Was that how Myer Hafetz's testimony had showed up there?

By then, though, I'd had enough for one night. I looked over at Rochester. "Our last night of being temporary bachelors," I said, as he lay on his side, his golden flanks rising and falling. "Do you miss Mama Lili?"

He sat up.

"Is that a yes?"

Rick called as I was rubbing Rochester's tummy. "My buddy told me that all the cold case files were digitized by a non-profit agency but right after that budget cuts came through, and the squad got scaled back, focusing only on cases in the last twenty years."

"Can he get you the digital file?"

"He gave me the name of the group and I looked at their website. In order to request the file I'd need a subpoena, and you and I both know we don't have enough to convince a judge to open that investigation."

"What's the name of the website?" "Steve."

"I just want to look," I said, though I knew I was lying.

Did Rick know, too? He hesitated for a moment, then blew out a deep breath. "It's called the Agency for Records Digitization. But Steve. You cannot hack into them. Do you hear me? That is illegal and I cannot be involved and I don't want my best friend to get arrested and sent back to prison."

"I guarantee you, I don't want that either," I said. He was right; hacking into the site was a very bad idea and I couldn't jeopardize everything I'd built in the last two years. "I give you my word, I won't hack their site."

"Good."

I ended the call. It wasn't illegal to do some research on the organization, though. To prove to myself that I was going to keep my word to Rick, I left the old laptop with my hacking tools in the attic, and used the legitimate computer to search.

There was very little online about the ARD beyond a contact

Dog Is in the Details

button, a log in for law enforcement officials and a mission statement that read: "To assist law enforcement by providing digitization services for paper files relating to unsolved crimes from the distant and recent past. Advances in forensic technology and evidence analysis may lead to the solution of cases that could not be properly investigated at the time of commission."

I went back to my search results. If I was interested in hacking this site, maybe someone else on the dark web had wanted to also – and didn't have the same legal or ethical restrictions I did.

There is a lot of information out there that doesn't come up in search results. Experts call that the "deep web" – things like your bank information, your medical records, anything that requires a log in and ID to retrieve. If you pull them up yourself, it's not illegal. But if others do, that's a whole different story.

There is another part of the deep web called the dark web – the place where hackers and crackers and script kiddies hang out, those who are interested in getting into those places where you ought to have permission. It's where I find my hacker tools, where I visit forums to keep up my skills, and where all manner of nefarious deeds take place, from supplying fake ID to money laundering and more.

It took some digging but eventually I found a forum dedicated to the Agency for Records Digitization. There were a lot of wild theories bandied about there – it was a front for the FBI or the CIA, further evidence of Big Brother's incursion into our lives, and so on. Several hackers had tried to break in, with varying levels of success, and I found after some more digging that I could access the records they'd found.

So I wasn't hacking, I told myself. I was just using my talents for discovering information that was out there to be found.

Whatever. My fingers were itching as I dove in the database that had been unlocked and reposted on a quasi-public site. The interface was rudimentary, very Web 1.0, with a simple search box and a button to click – not even the icon of a magnifying glass to glamorize your experience.

I typed in "Sapinsky" and clicked the button. I didn't realize I was holding my breath until a single record popped up: Sapinsky, Morris, underlined and hyperlinked.

I clicked on the link and was taken to a simple list of documents, each one a PDF file which could be read or downloaded. I saved each of them to a folder on my laptop, then exited the site.

Adrenaline was coursing through my system. I hadn't hacked in the sense that I hadn't broken through any security measures set up by the ADR to prevent access to their data. All I'd done was benefit from someone else's illegal act. I knew from reading legal opinions on the Wikileaks material that downloading and reading public available material was unlikely to be viewed as a crime unless you used material to steal someone's identity or commit a collateral crime. Would Rick see it the same way? Good thing I was no longer on parole, so I didn't have to worry about what my parole officer would say—or what he could have done to me if he'd discovered something like this on his watch.

Chapter 19
Big Questions

It was only nine o'clock, still early enough to pay an impromptu visit to Rick. "How'd you like to go for a ride?" I asked Rochester. "Go see your buddy Rascal?"

Rochester recognized the key words in that sentence and began hopping around like a demented kangaroo. I thought I'd get a better response from Rick if I came carrying beer, so we made a pit stop on the way to pick up a six-pack of Dogfish Head. I parked in Rick's driveway and then stepped up to his door, ringing the bell while holding the six-pack in one hand and my laptop in the other.

He opened the door and Rochester rushed past. He looked at the beer and the computer, then back up at me. "This does not bode well."

"All legal," I said. "I promise."

He blew out a long breath. "You'd better come in, then."

He popped the tops off a couple of beers for us while I turned on the laptop and opened the file directory. When he joined me at the kitchen table I explained to him how I'd found the files.

"So someone else hacked the site before you did," he said. "And you think that makes it okay."

I used the Wikileaks analogy.

"That material was sent to the news media and posted everywhere," Rick said. "You had to go digging for this."

"I did. But I didn't break any laws to find it. If anyone committed a criminal act it was whoever did the original hack. And I have no knowledge of who that was or how they did it."

He frowned at me and thought for a while. "Fine, let's see what you've got."

Morris Jacob Sapinsky was a white male, age 31, with a home address in Trenton. His occupation was Rabbi, his death was classified "violent," and the box that read "found dead" was also checked.

We read the description of the body and the visible wounds. Sapinsky had been shot in the chest by a small-caliber handgun. Stippling was observed around the wound, consistent with a shooter at close range. The manner of death was homicide, and an autopsy had been performed. The file was signed by the county medical examiner.

The investigating detective was a man named Bernard Parker. He had spoken with a man who discovered Sapinsky's body in the temple when he arrived for morning services, then called the police. In addition to that man, who spoke little English, Parker interviewed a number of men who had been at the evening *minyan*, or worship service, with the rabbi.

Only one man provided any information. Sandor Rabinowitz, aged 52, a native of Hungary now residing in Trenton, said that Rabbi Sapinsky had been attempting to build bridges between new immigrants and more established residents. This effort had been controversial, resulting in many arguments among members of Shomrei Torah.

Parker added that he spoke with a young boy named Solly, who had been studying with the rabbi that evening. He had a feeling that the boy knew something, but was too frightened to speak up, and Solly's parents either didn't speak English, or pretended not to.

He concluded his report with his belief that the rabbi had been killed due to this controversy, and that the insularity of the Jewish community would prevent an outside investigator from discovering the perpetrator.

"You believe this?" Rick asked me, when we'd read through everything.

"It doesn't seem reasonable that a Jew would kill his rabbi for doing charitable work. Even if members of the congregation were upset, they'd fire the rabbi before killing him."

"But it was an insular community, wasn't it?" Rick asked. "So it's possible that no one was willing to speak to this detective, and he made a conclusion based on the only facts that he had at hand."

Rochester and Rascal had been snoozing in the kitchen doorway, but Rochester woke up then and came over to me and woofed. "What do you want, boy?" I asked.

"He probably wants a treat," Rick said. He stood up and opened the jar in the shape of a dog where he kept biscuits, and Rascal recognized the sound and jumped up, too.

He gave each of the dogs a treat, and I marveled at how easily our dogs could communicate with us without actually speaking.

"There might have been a language problem, too," I said. "I'll bet most of the more recent immigrants didn't speak much English so it was hard for Parker to interview them."

Rick nodded. "They didn't have interpreters back then either. This is all you found?" "Yes."

"Show me how you found this information."

I went back to the deep web database where the hacker had posted what he'd retrieved from the Agency for Records Digitization, and typed into the search box. But Rochester was nosing my elbow and made me hit the enter key before finishing the rabbi's last name, sending a request for "Sapins" instead of Sapinsky.

This time, two results came up – the one I'd found earlier, and a second one called Hafetz, Meyer.

"That's the guy who wrote the Holocaust survivor document," I said. "At least, I think it's the same guy—the name is spelled a little differently."

I clicked the link and downloaded a folder similar to the one on Sapinsky. The first document was another medical examiner form, dated about a month before Sapinsky's death. Hafetz, too, had been killed by a shot at close range from a small caliber weapon. One of those whom the detective spoke to was a Rabbi Sapinski.

My brain was buzzing with connections and I had to stop reading and pull out the translation Daniel Epstein had prepared for me. It was dated September 12, 1948. Then I looked back at the ME's form, and pointed it out to Rick. "Hafetz was killed a month after he wrote up this document."

"You think there's a connection?"

I went back to the rabbi's file. "See here? Another month later, the rabbi is murdered. Two dates that match could be a coincidence, but not three."

Rick sat back in his chair. "You know when Hafetz came to Trenton?"

"According to the document that Epstein translated, Hafetz spent a year in a displaced persons camp in the American zone in Germany after he was liberated from Auschwitz in January, 1945. Then he made a connection with a relative in New York who sponsored him to come to the States. Probably no earlier than some time in 1946."

"So Hafetz comes here, then dictates his testimony in September, 1948. A month later he's killed outside the junkyard where he worked. Then a month after that, the rabbi is also shot dead in his synagogue. Anything after that?"

"Not that I know of."

"Any connection between Hafetz and the rabbi?"

"Both Jews, both living in Trenton. It was a small community then. And the rabbi worked at the Hebrew Sheltering Home, helping refugees. So it's a reasonable assumption that they knew each other."

"Which still doesn't get us anywhere in the present."

"Suppose after Hafetz dictated this document he gave it to the rabbi," I said. "Then Hafetz was killed, and the rabbi was worried, so he hid the document in the wall at the old shul."

"I can give you that. Then what?"

"Whoever killed Hafetz discovered the rabbi knew about the document, and killed him, too."

"Why?"

"That part I don't know. But then Joel found the document when he was camping out at the old shul. Totally random, I know. But that opened this old wound, whatever it is."

"But we're talking about something that happened almost sixty years ago," Rick said.

"There's no statute of limitations on murder. Suppose there was something else at the shul, some other document or connection to the two murders, and Joel Goldberg found it while he was sleeping there. If it was hidden behind the Belgian block wall like the photos were, no one would have known to remove them when the synagogue moved, or before the demolition started."

"Why would he do that?"

"I've been reading through Joel's emails, and it's clear he was obsessed with the Holocaust," I said. "And you yourself said that it's hard to know what's going on in the mind of someone with schizophrenia."

"Let's go back to the stuff about Hafetz's death," Rick said, and we looked again at the information from the digitized file. Hafetz's body had been discovered in an alley next to the junkyard where he worked, and the detective – Parker again – had assumed that someone had tried to rob Hafetz, and in the scuffle Hafetz had been killed.

"Well, this answers one question you had," I said, once I located that reference to Rabbi Sapinksi. "The rabbi and Hafetz knew each other. Since immigrants were less trusting of authority, it's reasonable that Hafetz took his suspicions to the rabbi rather than the police. Sapinsky even told Parker that he had discussed the Holocaust many times with Hafetz, trying to counsel him and help him recover from his trauma."

"I can't imagine going through something like that," Rick said. "How can you go back to ordinary life after you've lived through what these people did? Seeing your friends and family slaughtered, being subjected to such awful conditions?"

"We spent all of eight grade in Sunday school studying the Holocaust," I said. "The big question was where was God when all this stuff was happening to his chosen people."

"And the answer?"

"There is no one answer." I tried to put myself back in that classroom in the school building at Shomrei Torah. Those small wooden desks, the chalkboard at the front of the room, the way the late afternoon light slanted in through the windows that looked out at the railroad tracks, the way our teacher had to pause when a loaded train came by and shook the walls.

"Some people said that God abandoned the Jews," I said finally. "Others said it was his way of testing us to make sure that we still believed in him."

"What do you think?"

"I thought a lot about God after Mary had the first miscarriage," I said. "How could he do this to us? How could he kill that innocent baby?" I felt my voice choking up as I remembered the horror of that time. "I went to services a couple of times after that, out in California, and I spoke to the rabbi there. He reminded me that God moves in mysterious ways, that it wasn't all about me, or Mary, or the baby. That there were larger forces at work in the world, that we were all part of that."

Rochester got back up from the floor, stretched his paws in front of him and yawned, then came over to nuzzle my knee. I stroked his soft fur, glad that I had him in my life.

"And did that help?" Rick asked.

"Eventually. When I was in prison, I recognized that Mary and I didn't belong together, and having a child wasn't going to solve the problems between us. That maybe this was God's way of telling us that."

"Ouch."

"Yeah, I didn't like that idea, that this tiny baby had to suffer because of us. But I had a lot of time on my hands then, and I started to read bits of the Bible and the commentary, and I realized that the rabbi I'd spoken to was right. It wasn't about us, or the baby. That God is not vindictive, or benevolent. He – or she – just is. And as long as we believe, we have to keep moving forward."

"I still go to St. Ignatius sometimes, you know," Rick said. That was the Catholic church in Yardley. "And every now and then the priest will say something that resonates with me. That God handles divine justice, but that we are responsible for earthly justice. It's why we have police and courts and prisons."

There didn't seem to be much more we could do then, so I closed up my laptop. "Good job finding that information," Rick said as I did. "And I'm glad you didn't have to hack into anywhere to find it."

"I'm doing my best to stay on the straight and narrow," I said. "Though I have to admit, it's not always easy."

"That's what makes us human," Rick said. "Knowing the wrong that we can do, and resisting it."

Chapter 20
Duty and Family

Before I left for work on Thursday morning, I put a piece of brisket in the slow cooker, along with some potatoes and carrots, so that there'd be a warm welcome home dinner for Lili by the time she returned.

We drove up to Friar Lake, where I met with Joey Capodilupo, answered emails, and filled out a lot of college forms relating to the agreement to rent out our facilities to the group represented by Professor Backus.

I took Rochester out for a walk around Friar Lake when I was finished. I missed Lili, and it was hard to remember how I'd functioned as a single man. Well, I hadn't done all that well, at least not until Rochester had come into my life and given me his unconditional love, as well as the need to feed, groom, walk and play with him.

Back when I was married, I'd relished Mary's occasional business trips for the chance to be on my own, and it was always a bit of a letdown when she returned home. Guess that should have told me something. We left for the airport soon after that, and once again I blasted Springsteen through the Bluetooth connection to my phone. Let Bruce wash all my cares away.

As I neared the airport I saw a skinny black shirtless guy, his torso covered with tattoos, walking along the verge waving at passing cars. Another homeless guy like Joel Goldberg? Or just a free spirit?

I expected Lili to be happy to be home and away from her mother's demands, but she didn't look all that pleased when she got into the car. Of course she leaned over and kissed my cheek, and scratched behind Rochester's ears, but I could tell there was something wrong.

It's the eternal conundrum between couples. Do you poke and prod for the source of the pain, risking an explosion? Or wait for your significant other to open up, with the possibility that she'll think you uncaring because you didn't ask?

Fortunately, Rochester helped me out. From the back seat, he kept woofing and leaning forward to sniff Lili until finally her bad mood evaporated. Good dog.

"I don't know what I'm going to do," she said eventually, as we sped up the highway toward home. "My mother needs more than I can give."

Another one of those booby-trapped comments, and I had to tread carefully. I remembered the rabbi's commentary about the first fruits of the harvest offered at the Temple, the idea that you gave back to the one who had given you life – either God, or your mother. "You love her," I said. "The most important thing you can do is let her know that."

"But who's going to help her out when she goes back to her apartment?" Lili asked. "We can hire an aide, but how can I be sure that person can be trusted to take care of her? What happens when she falls again? Is it fair to shift all the burden to Fedi and Sara? She took care of both of us for years, decades even. Don't I owe her that same duty?"

"Duty's a heavy word," I said. "In the end, what's our duty to each other? You know my favorite definition of Judaism."

"The one from Rabbi Hillel?"

"Exactly." Rabbi Hillel, one of the early Jewish sages, had been challenged to state the essence of Judaism while standing on one food. He had said, "Love thy neighbor as thyself."

"And what does that have to do with my mother?" Lili demanded.

"That you love her as you love yourself. You recognize that she has good and bad points, just like each of us does. And that your love for her has to be equal to your love for yourself. You don't owe it to her to turn your whole life upside down to take care of her—just to make sure that she's safe, and well-cared for, that she has a roof over her head, food in her belly, and that she knows you love her."

"You've been hanging around with that rabbi," Lili said, but she smiled. "That sounds like a very Talmudic observation."

"And a selfish one," I admitted. "I love you and I only want the best for you. I don't want you to be torn up over what happens to your mother, just to be happy that you've done all you can."

"But is this all? Occasional visits, telephone support? She gave me and Fedi a home, after all. Shouldn't I do the same for her?"

"She already has a home," I said gently. "You told me yourself, she loves her apartment and she doesn't want to move out of it. You were infants, and then kids, and you couldn't fend for yourselves, so she had to take care of you. Now you've got this balancing act to handle, letting her do as much as she can for herself, and then picking up the slack between you and your brother."

"Sounds good in theory," she said. Then she turned toward the window and we didn't speak again for the rest of the trip.

The brisket was tender by the time we got home, the aroma filling the house with warmth and welcome. I threw a loaf of frozen garlic bread into the microwave, opened a bottle of wine, and we sat in the kitchen and ate in a companionable silence. I had missed Lili while she was gone, and I was glad to have her home. I told her so, and she said she was happy to be back home, too, even if it meant she had left things hanging in Florida.

We were relaxing on the sofa, our feet entwined as we read, when Lili asked, "Did Rick propose to Tamsen yet?"

"Don't know. The only thing we've been talking about is murder."

"Do you think Rick is stalling?"

For a moment I thought she was talking about the investigations into the two murders. Then I realized she wondered about his proposal to Tamsen.

"He's got a lot on his plate right now," I said. "Lots of petty crimes in town, and this murder, too. If I were him, I'd want to wait until I could give Tamsen my full attention." "I just hope he doesn't wait too long."

I turned to look at her. "Why? You think Tamsen might get impatient and break up with him?"

"I'm sure I'm just projecting. But both Philip and Adriano proposed to me on the spur of the moment, and both times I accepted without thinking too much. If we'd waited, I might have seen the warning signs and never agreed to get married."

"Rick sends off warning signs?"

She pushed at my side. "Don't go interpreting too much. Both of them have baggage, and if something big comes up before they're committed, who knows what might happen. Suppose Justin gets sick, or Tamsen does. Or Rick gets hurt on the job. Or that crazy ex-wife of his comes back to mess up his life again."

I slid onto my side so I was facing her. "We're good, though, aren't we?"

"What do you mean?"

"I'm here for you whatever happens with your mother," I said. "In sickness and in health, for richer or poorer, all that stuff. We don't need a ceremony or legal paperwork to confirm that, right?"

She leaned in and kissed me. "I love you, Steve Levitan. Things feel different with you from what I felt with Philip or Adriano. Like we're in this for the long haul. So yes, I agree with you, we're good, and we don't need anyone else to confirm that."

We kissed again, and then Rochester scrambled up between us, eager to get in on the love fest. We laughed and pushed him away, and then got busy demonstrating that commitment we felt.

Chapter 21
Who is Sylvia

Lili warned me Friday morning that she'd probably be at her office all day catching up on work. "Don't count on me for dinner. I'll grab a sandwich or something."

"I was thinking I'd go back to Shomrei Torah tonight," I said. "I want to ask Rabbi Goldberg about the document that I found at the old shul, see if his brother might have been able to understand it. I'll feed and walk the hound before I go."

She kissed me goodbye and went upstairs to shower and dress for work, and Rochester and I left the house a few minutes later. On my way to Friar Lake, Henry Namias called my cell. "Daniel Epstein left me a message I should talk to you," he said. "Of course, now that I call him back, he doesn't answer. What am I supposed to talk about?"

I explained about the testimony found by Joel Goldberg. "I understand you knew Myer Hafetz."

"Who told you that? Epstein? What a mouth he has on him."

"I also read a story you told my mother for the Oral History Project," I said. "Maybe you remember her? Her name was Sylvia Gordon before she married my father."

"Sheindeleh Gordon! Of course I remember her. You're her son? Why didn't you say so?"

I hadn't heard anyone call my mother by her Yiddish nickname in years. Her aunts and uncles called her that when I was a kid, and my father often used it as a term of either endearment or frustration. "I didn't think you'd remember her," I said. "Could I talk to you about what you remember about Myer Hafetz? And my mother, too. I lost her too early."

"What a shame," he said. "I was at the funeral. Is your father still alive?"

"He passed a couple of years ago," I said, grateful that Namias didn't remember my father's service, or that I hadn't been able to attend because I was incarcerated. "Are you going to be at Shomrei Torah tonight?"

"Where else would I be? You want to talk after services? A little Shabbos wine goes a long way to opening up the memories."

I agreed that I'd see him that evening. I remembered when I was a kid I'd stumbled on a book of translations of English songs and poems into Yiddish. There was "Affen Shpitz Alten Smoky," or "On top of Old Smoky," and one that had a particular resonance— Shakespeare's short poem, "Who is Silvia?"

I had immediately looked up the poem's text in a Shakespeare compendium I'd found in our basement – one of my mother's old college textbooks. The poem became one of my favorites, because I adored my mother and at that age, she could do no wrong, and because her named matched in both English and Yiddish.

Who was my mother, anyway? A devout Jewish woman, in her way. We never kept kosher, but she and my father fasted on Yom Kippur for years, they observed the Yahrzeits of their parents, and she chauffeured me to Sunday school and Hebrew school for years.

She spent her working life as a bookkeeper and secretary, read voraciously, and loved to garden. So little to sum up a life, and yet I was pretty sure she'd been happy with what she accomplished. A comfortable home, a loving marriage, an educated son.

Like Victor Namias had described his wife Esther, my mother was a *balabusta*, a woman born to run the world. She volunteered at

Shomrei Torah, chaired the Lakes Garden Club, looked after her elderly relatives, ran our household.

And yet none of those things got to the essence of who she was. Do we ever really know our parents, no matter how much time we spend with them, how much we analyze their behavior?

Those ideas continued to circle around in my head until I left Friar Lake around four, fed and walked Rochester, and then went to Shabbat services at Shomrei Torah. Daniel Epstein wasn't at the door greeting congregants, and I didn't see him in the pews either. I hoped he wasn't feeling under the weather. I ought to give him a call, take Rochester over for a visit. I'd seen how the attentions of my generous golden had made Epstein look better.

After the service was over, I approached Rabbi Goldberg, and I realized I had barely paid attention to the sermon, my mind full of my parents and my own history.

But I wanted to talk about his brother, not his sermon. "That document I found at the old shul was a testimony from the Yad Vashem holocaust center," I said. "Would Joel have recognized the Hebrew name of the center at the top of the page?"

"I think so," the rabbi said. "Like me, Joel took years of Hebrew and he often went to temple with me and our parents after his bar mitzvah. So he certainly knew the alphabet. And as I think I told you, he was very interested in the Holocaust, to the point where he was convinced that America was at risk of another one. All the political name-calling and putting blame on immigrants. He was afraid that if the wrong people got into power, they'd start going after the Jews again."

He sighed. "I know it was paranoia from his illness, but I can't help believing there was some truth in what he believed."

Another congregant came over to speak to the rabbi, and I found Henry Namias by the platter of petit fours, a plastic cup of wine in his hand.

"So you're Sylvia Gordon's boy," he said. "I haven't thought of her in a long time. A very smart young woman, a real go-getter." He leaned forward and peered at my face. "You look like her, a little. The nose and mouth."

"I've been told that," I said.

"She was four years younger than I was," Namias said. "I knew her from shul and I was excited when she asked to interview my father. I convinced him to say yes."

"I read the transcript," I said. "Daniel Epstein saved it. Did you know him when you were a boy, too?"

"Only by name. He's much older than I am, you know. Six years. A lot to kids."

"He told me that you knew a man named Myer Hafetz. That you might be able to tell me something about him."

"Cousin Myer? What do you care about a man dead fifty, sixty years ago?"

I explained about the testimony I'd found at the old shul, though I didn't mention it was Rochester who'd nosed it out. "I was fascinated and I wanted to know more about him."

"I think I was ten years old when he came to stay with us. I don't know how he was connected – maybe a landsman, maybe a distant cousin of my mother's. He was German and had been in Auschwitz and he used to sit for hours talking to my mother in Yiddish and broken English. My father gave him a job at our family junkyard on New Street, and in the evening, after he had finished work and we had all had dinner, he told me stories of the old country so I could help him with his English."

Henry Namias got a faraway look in his eyes and I could see he was remembering those years. "He was a real raconteur, and Berlin before the war came alive in his stories. He was a very clever man, and he was able to evade the Nazis for years, hiding in abandoned houses, scavenging for food. One day he was so hungry that he dared to go out in the daytime, and he was stopped and the police demanded he drop his pants to see if he was circumcised. As soon as they saw, they arrested him, and he was sent to Auschwitz, with the rest of the Jews from Berlin."

I couldn't help shivering. What must that have been like, living in constant fear? Most boys born around the time I was in the United States were circumcised, so my missing foreskin wasn't as clear a symbol of my Jewish identity as it would have been for a German Jew in the 1940s. How would I have felt, being forced to drop my pants on a public street, knowing what it would reveal?

"He was lucky," Namias continued. "He was young and strong and they put him to work, and the war ended before they could wear him out and gas him. He felt like God had saved him for a reason, to tell his story. That's why he filled out that form from Yad Vashem." He peered at me. "You read Yiddish?"

I shook my head. "I had Daniel Epstein translate it for me." I paused for a moment. "How long did Hafetz stay with you?"

"Only a few months," Namias said. "Then one night he didn't come home for dinner, and my mother sent me over to New Street to get him. The junkyard was locked up and I was confused. Where was cousin Myer? I called his name but he didn't answer, so I started looking around. When I went into the alley beside the building I found him there, on the ground."

His voice quavered as he remembered. "I kneeled down and shook him but he didn't wake up. There was blood coming out of his belly and I got some on my hands. I ran home like I was on fire and when my mother saw the blood she nearly fainted. She sent my father to the junkyard and she cleaned me up."

He looked me in the eyes. "That was the last time I saw Cousin Myer."

Chapter 22
Hardy Boys

As I left the synagogue with Rochester I felt a chill—maybe from the cold air, or more likely from the story Henry Namias had told me. No one had been willing to tell him what happened to Hafetz when he was a boy, and by the time he was an adult he'd pushed away the dark memory of discovering the body.

When I got home I went back over the police detective's report on the death of Myer Hafetz. There was no mention of a boy discovering the body, and I assumed that the Namiases had kept their son out of the investigation. What else wasn't mentioned? There was no way to know.

By the time we returned from Shomrei Torah, Lili was home, and I pushed aside all thoughts of murder, past and present, to be there with her and my puppy.

Saturday morning I took Rochester for a long walk, then snuggled back into bed beside Lili and dozed. Around ten, my phone trilled with Rick's ring tone. Lili was closest to the phone so she reached for it. "I wonder if he proposed," she said as she pressed the button to answer.

"No, it's Lili," she said. "Have you asked her yet?"

He said something that appeared to be no, and she continued,

"What are you waiting for? I thought you were going to do it this week."

She listened for a moment, then said, with a deep sigh, "Oy. Here's your brother from another mother." She handed the phone to me. "Another murder. And I thought Stewart's Crossing was such a safe little town when I agreed to move in with you."

"What happened?" I asked Rick.

"The man who did that translation for you. What was his name again?"

"Daniel Epstein. Why?"

He groaned. "I thought that was it. I'm afraid someone made sure that Mr. Epstein would no longer be with us. I'm here at his house in Crossing Estates. Maid came in to clean this morning and discovered the body. Fortunately she called 911 before she started to clean up."

"You're going to find my fingerprints there," I said. "I spent a couple of hours at Epstein's house on Wednesday morning, going through some of his old files."

"Did you clean up after yourself?"

"What are you, my mother? Of course I did. Why would you ask something like that?"

"Because it looks like the person who killed Epstein ransacked his house, in particular his office on the second floor. Files dumped out, papers scattered everywhere."

"You want me to come over there? I can help you sort through everything."

"I can't do that, Steve. Because your prints are going to be in the house, and in that office, I have to consider you a suspect."

"Me!"

"Look, I know you, and I very much doubt you drove over to this old man's house, hit him over the head, and ransacked his office. I wish I could use your help, but I have to play this one by the book."

My stomach roiled. Daniel Epstein was dead, and I was one of the last people to see him alive. Though he was elderly and somewhat frail, when I'd spoken with him he had been lively and animated. I'd visited his house, looked through his files, become a part of his life—and now he was dead.

"Here's what you can do," Rick said. "Make a full inventory of the material you took away from Epstein's house. Maybe you have what Epstein's murderer was looking for."

Great. In a flash I had gone from suspected killer to potential victim.

"You think it's someone from Shomrei Torah?"

"I'm not making any assumptions. Both Mr. Epstein and Joel Goldberg were connected to that synagogue, and my coincidence radar is ringing. But it is possible that the two deaths are unrelated, and I'm going to investigate every angle I find."

I heard him speak to someone in the house with him, and then he came back on the line and said he'd come over when he was finished.

Rochester clambered up onto the bed and slumped down beside me, his head resting on my chest. "Who's Daniel Epstein?" Lili asked. "You look very pale."

"A very nice older man from the Talmud study group at Shomrei Torah," I said. "He's the one who translated that piece in Yiddish for me."

"Sometimes I worry about you, Steve. People around you have a nasty habit of dying."

"I hardly knew the man," I protested. "I met him at Talmud study, and then Rabbi Goldberg suggested him as a translator."

"And?"

"And I went to his house with Rochester." "Who Rick calls the Death Dog."

Rochester nuzzled me. "You don't like that nickname," I said as I scratched behind his ears. "Uncle Rick is just jealous of your crime-solving abilities."

I explained what Rick had told me, and that I'd have to go through Epstein's files.

"Did he have a family?"

I told her what I knew about Epstein's life. "He sounds like a very nice man, and it sounds like he lived well," she said. "Try to remember that. My father would have called him a *tzadik*, a righteous man. We should all live to be remembered that way."

"You're right. And he deserves to have justice for his death."

"You're going to go need a good breakfast," Lili said. "How about a cheese and mushroom omelet with a side of bacon?"

Rochester's ears perked up, whether because he heard breakfast or bacon.

"That would be awesome," I said. "There's a roll of those quick-bake biscuits in the fridge, too."

"Don't push your luck, Hardy Boy," she said, but she smiled. "Come on, Rochester. Let's go make breakfast."

I appreciated Lili's offer, but I thought calling me a Hardy Boy was a little harsh, not just because a man I had met and liked was dead. It was one thing for Rick or me to call ourselves the Hardy Boys, but when Lili used the term it sounded demeaning, like we were kids playing at crime-solving. There were bad people out there, and Rick was one of the bulwarks who protected society from them. I was honored to be able to help now and then.

I took a quick shower and got dressed, and by the time I got downstairs Lili had breakfast on the table. "What's on your agenda today?" I asked.

"I'm meeting Tamsen for a mani-pedi at eleven," she said. "I need a little pampering after all that aggravation in Florida."

She left a short time later, and after I cleaned up the kitchen I sat down at the dining room table with my laptop and all of the files I'd taken from Daniel Epstein's house. I opened a new spreadsheet and began cataloguing everything.

Every now and then I'd stop and consider. Was it this file that the murderer had been looking for? This article, this clipping, this photograph?

It all seemed so harmless to me, from so long ago. I saved the information on Rabbi Sapinsky's murder for last. That had to be the connection, didn't it? Suppose the rabbi's killer was still alive, and believed that Epstein had incriminating evidence?

But all Epstein had saved were a few newspaper clippings.

Nothing that pointed to a particular individual.

I opened a new file and began to type. "Who is still alive who might have known Rabbi Sapinsky?"

I thought of the elderly men I knew from the Talmud study group. Aaron Feinberg, Saul Benesch and Henry Namias had been involved with Shomrei Torah for as long as I could remember. But had they worshipped at Shomrei Torah when they were younger?

Epstein had told me that he had celebrated his bar mitzvah there, the service officiated by Rabbi Sapinsky. I went back to the oral history Victor Namias had dictated to my mother and scanned through it. Toward the end, I found a mention that because there was no Sephardic congregation in Trenton, Namias and his family had joined Shomrei Torah at Esther Namias's urging.

So Henry Namias had to have known the rabbi. But he was only ten years old—way too young to have committed murder.

He was the one who had discovered Myer Hafetz's body, though. So he was connected to both victims. Could his father have been the killer? Namias had told me that his mother and Myer Hafetz were close, spending hours together speaking Yiddish. What if Victor had gotten jealous and killed his rival? And then the rabbi found out, and had to be silenced as well?

Pure speculation. And even if it was true, what would have prompted Namias to kill Joel Goldberg and Daniel Epstein? His father was long dead.

I had finished my inventory by the time Rick arrived. He brought Rascal with him, and the dogs immediately began to romp together, chasing each other's tails around the living room. I went into the kitchen to get tumblers of ice water for both of us, and when I returned to the living room, Rick was on the floor with both dogs jumping on him. He was laughing and scratching them, but when I came in he sobered up and stood.

"When was the last time you saw Daniel Epstein?" he asked.

"I joined this discussion group at Shomrei Torah a couple of weeks ago. We meet in the rabbi's study on Wednesday mornings. After the session was over I spoke to Epstein and asked him if he knew anything about the death of Rabbi Sapinsky, back in the forties. He told me that he had a lot of files and invited me to his house to look through them."

I scratched behind Rochester's ears. "I followed him to his house, and I was there until about noon on Wednesday. Do you know when he was killed?"

"The ME will have to do an autopsy. The air conditioning was on in the house and the body was cold, so it's hard to speculate, but at least a day or so."

"Were there any signs of forced entry?"

Rick shook his head. "No broken windows, no pry marks on any door. So I'm assuming that Mr. Epstein knew his killer and let him into the house."

Rick had spoken to Epstein's son and daughter. Neither of them knew anyone with a motive to kill their father, nor did they believe that their father kept anything in the house worth killing for. "He had a floor safe in the upstairs bedroom with some gold coins, legal papers and a couple hundred bucks in cash, but the safe wasn't opened," Rick said.

"Do you have an inventory of what was stolen?"

"Not completely. The son is meeting me at the house tomorrow morning to go over the list the cleaning lady and I put together and see what else we can add to it."

"He hire any handymen or other workers in the last few weeks or months?"

"I'll be going over that with his son."

We went through the inventory of the files I had taken from Epstein's house. "Nothing seems that damaging to anyone who's alive today," I said. I showed him the list I'd begun, of who might have known Rabbi Sapinsky.

"What about these other two men," Rick asked. "Benesch and Feinberg?"

"I don't know. I was thinking I'd try and speak with each of them, maybe at the study group, or maybe at Daniel Epstein's funeral."

"Just be careful. From everything I've heard, Mr. Epstein was a kind man without enemies. If one of those men killed Epstein, you don't want to put yourself in his sights."

Chapter 23
A Place to Rest

The ME expedited the autopsy and released Daniel Epstein's body quickly so that his funeral could be held on Sunday morning, graveside services in the same cemetery in Trenton where my parents were buried.

It was a gray day, and a restless wind scattered dead leaves along the gravel paths between sections of the cemetery. I parked and headed toward the green awning in the oldest section, where aged granite tombstones, faded after years in all weathers, stood erect over the final resting places of generations of Trenton's Jewish dead.

Epstein's son and daughter, along with their families, took the seats in front of the open grave, and Saul Benesch and Henry Namias sat behind them, along with other elderly people I assumed were Epstein's contemporaries and friends. I stood in the back beside a woman I recognized from the Talmud study group.

Rabbi Goldberg gave a brief eulogy, focusing on Daniel Epstein's dedication to his family, his heritage and his synagogue. Then Epstein's son spoke about the example his father had set for him.

My eyes teared up and I wondered about my father's funeral. Had anyone spoken in my place? Had my cousins been there, had they wondered about my absence?

One by one, Epstein's family and close friends stepped up to sprinkle dirt over the coffin, and I had to turn away because of how deeply the experience affected me. I had not been there to speed my father along on his journey to the afterlife, and I would forever feel that pain.

I stood beside an elaborate tombstone dedicated to Philip Gross, "husband, father, grandfather and Holocaust survivor." Beneath it was inscribed "Never Forget." I heard the sound of the Kaddish prayer, and then the gears grinding as Epstein's coffin was lowered into the ground, quiet sobbing coming from the family.

It was difficult to compose myself, and I took a couple of deep breaths and wiped the tears away from my eyes. I turned to find Saul Benesch approaching me. He wore a khaki trenchcoat over a dark suit, and he seemed somehow smaller than I remembered.

"It's a terrible thing," he said. "We're not safe in our own houses anymore."

"Did you know Mr. Epstein for a long time?"

"From the old days," he said. "I had trouble with the Hebrew for my Torah portion, and he coached me. He was a mensch, even back then."

"Was this at Shomrei Torah?" I asked.

Benesch nodded. "I was raised Orthodox, but my wife, may she rest in peace, was an *Italianer*, a Catholic. The only rabbi who would marry us was the one at Shomrei Torah, so we joined here."

"The Jewish community back then must have been very close," I said. "Did you know Mr. Feinberg back then, too?"

He shook his head. "Aaron? He's a baby. I knew his father of blessed memory—he was a big *macher* at Shomrei Torah when my wife and I joined. But Aaron is fifteen years younger than I am. It wasn't until he came home from college and got involved in the temple that I got to know him."

The family left the gravesite and began to walk toward their limo. "You're going to the son's house for shiva?"

I shook my head. "I don't... I can't..."

Benesch put his hand on my shoulder. "It's all right," he said. "We each grieve in our own way."

I watched him walk slowly back toward the line of parked cars, and then turned to walk toward where my parents were buried. When my mother passed away, my father bought a joint headstone and had everything engraved on it except his date of death. He had also bought a pre-need package that paid for all the expenses of a coffin, opening the grave and so on.

I thought it was morbid at the time, but when he died I was grateful that I could handle everything long-distance. Now I stood in front of the grave and looked at the stone. "Levitan" was engraved at the top, with my father to the left and my mother to the right.

I realized that was the way they'd always slept in the wood-framed double bed they had bought, along with a whole bedroom suite, soon after they married.

A tilted water pitcher had been engraved above my father's name, with the words "Husband, Father" beneath it. Our last name implied that we were Levites, from the ancient clan whose members were responsible for washing the hands of the priests at the Temple in ancient days.

As is common for women, a candelabra was above my mother's first and maiden names – Sylvia Gordon – with "Wife, Mother" beneath it.

What would my stone say? I was no one's husband, no one's father. I wasn't a Holocaust survivor like Philip Gross. What would stand for my life?

My eyes teared up again. Where would I go, when my time came? A single plot there in the same cemetery? Would I be buried beside Lili? If we didn't marry, we'd need separate stones, wouldn't we? Was it too early to consider buying the plots?

Maybe Lili would want to be in a cemetery with her parents. Her father had been buried somewhere in Miami; I knew that she'd gone to visit his grave while she was there to look after her mother.

I shook off those grim thoughts. I found a pair of small pebbles and placed on one each side of my parents' headstone, in the Jewish custom. As I was walking back to my car, the rabbi intercepted me.

"Have you learned anything from Joel's emails?" he asked.

I told him about the man Joel had corresponded with, who went by the moniker NotwhoIthinkIam.

"From some details in his messages, I have the impression that this person lives somewhere in Trenton," I said. "Have you spoken to anyone in the congregation who had similar concerns?"

"Not that I can recall. Do you think this is the person who killed my brother?"

"That's a big leap, Rabbi," I said gently. "Right now I'm just following leads."

He nodded. "I appreciate that. It's just... officiating at this funeral, when Daniel Epstein died a violent death just like Joel, I can't help but think of him."

He looked at me as if the connection had suddenly appeared to him. "Do you think the same person could have killed both of them?"

"I don't know. There are certainly connections – for example, that document in Yiddish that I found in the ruins of Shomrei Torah, where Joel had been camping. Daniel translated it for me. But it's also possible that Daniel was the victim of some kind of home invasion, as scary as that sounds."

"It's times like this that I have to remind myself that everything that happens is part of God's grand plan," he said. "Even if His purposes are unclear to us."

I remembered my conversation with Rick about how a benevolent God could have allowed a tragedy like the Shoah to happen. "That's the definition of faith, isn't it?"

He smiled. "Maybe you should lead the Talmud study sometime."

"Oh, no, I'll leave that to you," I said. "You're continuing the group, aren't you?"

"Of course. I have to believe that it is what God would want."

We shook hands and he strode back to where the line of cars was snaking its way out of the cemetery.

I looked around me at all the graves and stones, those with an accumulation of pebbles on the top and those that looked like they had been ignored, that there was no one left to mourn those who had been interred there. I felt a sense of peace wash over me. The Jewish people had survived centuries of slavery, persecution and exile. Trenton, while by no means a garden of Eden, was at least a place where these souls could rest.

Could there be rest, though, for Daniel Epstein, for Joel Goldberg, Rabbi Sapinsky and Myer Hafetz, if we did not know the truth of what happened to them?

That, it occurred to me as I walked back to my car, was where I came in. Was I terminally nosy, as I often wondered? Or was the curiosity I felt about solving crimes really God's hand moving through me?

Either way, I still had more investigating to do.

Chapter 24
Good Men

When I got home from Daniel Epstein's funeral I went back to the file I'd created on my laptop and added in the information I'd gotten from Saul Benesch. He had known Daniel Epstein when they were children, both studying at Shomrei Torah, which meant he knew Rabbi Sapinsky.

Lili and I had plans to go out to dinner that evening with our friends Gail and Declan, so I pushed aside my research and we drove up to Le Canal, a French restaurant in New Hope. On the way I asked, "How is your mother today?"

"Complaining about the food at rehab. It has no flavor and there isn't enough of it. Sara has been making empanadas but they aren't as good as the ones my mother makes."

"So basically she's back to normal," I said. "That's good."

We met Gail and Declan in the parking lot. She was a young blonde in her late twenties who had grown up in Levittown, gone to the Culinary Institute of America, and snagged a prime job as a pastry chef in New York. When her mother was diagnosed with cancer, Gail had moved back to Bucks County to look after her, and eventually opened the Chocolate Ear café in the center of Stewart's Crossing.

Declan had known her back then, when he was an MBA student at Columbia, but she was dating his jerky roommate at the time, and he had to wait until she was free to make his move.

In New York, Gail had worked with the chef at Le Canal, and that connection was always good to get us comped something, an appetizer platter or a special dessert. And it was a lovely, romantic restaurant on the Delaware Canal, so it was good all around.

We sat at a four-top with a view of the river as evening drew around us. We chatted for a couple of minutes about the new dog-friendly annex Gail had added to the café, so that during the chill of winter or the heat of summer, you could spend time with your canine companion in comfort, avoiding health code restrictions about animals in food service areas.

The waiter brought out a platter of amuse-bouches, compliments of the chef -- small rectangles of grilled salmon crusted with peppercorns. After he left, Gail grimaced. "I hate to turn down a gift of food, but don't those look like little coffins?"

"You have a very active imagination," Declan said, and Lili shot me a sidelong look. That was a trait she felt I had as well.

"Sorry, but I just heard that one of my favorite customers passed away and his funeral was today."

"Not Daniel Epstein?" I didn't have the same compunction about the food, and I speared one of the salmon rectangles and put it on my plate.

"You know him?"

"It's a small town, my love," Declan said, in his Kiwi accent. "Haven't we figured out that everyone knows everyone else?"

"We're not quite that inbred," I said. "There are nearly ten thousand people in Stewart's Crossing and I doubt any of us know that big a percentage."

"But you knew Daniel?" Gail asked. "He used to come in the café quite often, always for a big mug of hot chocolate with sugar-free raspberry syrup, and a *pain aux raisins*."

I'd never had Gail's hot chocolate, but I'd tried the snail-shaped pastry studded with juicy raisins, so I figured Daniel Epstein had good taste.

"The last few times I saw him, he was looking more and more frail," Gail said. "So I guess his death shouldn't be a shock."

"He didn't die of old age." I lowered my voice. "He was killed during a burglary at his house in Crossing Estates."

Gail's mouth opened. "That's awful!" she said, and Declan took her hand. "Is Rick investigating?"

Rick and I often met at the Chocolate Ear, so both she and Declan knew him. "He is." I sliced a piece of the salmon and put it in my mouth. The peppery coating was a great contrast to the smoothness of the fish.

"I wonder," Gail said. "About what?" I asked.

"He met several times with this woman, and I was surprised – she didn't look like someone he would know."

"Why did you think that?"

"I don't know. She was young, only in her late teens or early twenties, an African-American woman with this elaborate hairstyle, a coil of braids on top of her head that reminded me of Medusa and her snakes."

I hadn't noticed anyone of that description at Epstein's funeral.

She shivered. "Maybe that was it, that evil-looking hairdo. I worried that maybe she was trying to romance Daniel or take advantage of him. He was such a good man."

The same term that Rabbi Goldberg had used to me – a good man. I hoped that my goodness, such as it was, wouldn't lead me to the same end as Daniel Epstein.

"You should tell Rick about her," I said. "I'm not saying she had any connection to his death, but I'm sure Rick wants to know everyone Daniel was in contact with recently."

Gail promised that she would, and we all focused on eating, and on more positive topics. Lili told us a funny story about Miami. Declan had been there on a business trip and he chimed in, and I zoned out for a bit, wondering when I would get to Miami and when I would meet Lili's mother.

Would I ever call Senora Weinstock my mother-in-law? I'd finally stopped calling Lili my girlfriend—I just introduced her, or mentioned her, and let whoever I was talking with draw their own conclusions. We weren't teenagers, after all, and the English language had yet to come up with an acceptable word for us to use. Companion sounded like a paid position, and partner was too businesslike. Most of the time it was used between same-sex couples.

Lili had suggested we use the Spanish terms *"novio"* and *"novia,"* which had a variety of meanings from fiancé to sweetheart. But this was Pennsylvania, and Spanish terms weren't as well-known as they might be in Miami.

After dinner, we walked out into the parking lot together, and I held Lili's hand. I'd enjoyed the meal and the chance to spend time with friends. But a chilly wind swept through the parking lot, reminding me that two men I had a tangential connection to had died recently. Would someone even closer to me be next?

It was seven-thirty the next morning, and I'd just gotten back from walking Rochester when my cell phone rang with Rick's tone. I stuck the phone to my ear as I juggled pouring Rochester's kibble into his bowl.

"Do me a favor?" Rick asked. His voice was raspy, as if he'd smoked a pack of cigarettes, though I knew he was too careful about his body to smoke. "I had to leave the house fast this morning and I didn't get a chance to feed Rascal."

"Sure. I can stop by on my way to work. Developments in a case?"

"Not exactly. I'm at St. Mary's Hospital in Langhorne. In the ER." He started to cough, and when he stopped he said, "My heart started going crazy this morning and I freaked out and called 911. They brought me here."

"Jesus, Rick. You should have called me. I'll feed Rascal and come right over there."

"You don't need to. They're just running some tests. The doc thinks it's just stress."

"Even so. You'll need a ride home when they're finished with you."

I scrambled upstairs, showered and dressed and told Lili where I was going. "Send him my love," she said.

With Rick out of action, I knew what I needed to do. Before I left the house I retrieved my laptop with the hacking tools from its hiding place in the attic. I knew there had to be clues somewhere to the two murders in the past – and perhaps how they connected to the two in the present. I was tired of resisting the temptation to hack my way to a solution online. I had these skills, and someone needed my help. I'd put my conscience aside and see what I could find.

I fed Rascal and left Rochester there with him to keep him company. Then I picked up I-95 in Yardley and headed inland toward Newtown. In high school, when I'd stayed late for speech and debate club or the math team, I'd ridden the late bus home. It followed a wide path around Newtown, Yardley and Stewart's Crossing, dropping off individual kids all around the area, and though I'd become familiar with all those back roads, many of them now were nearly unrecognizable as farms had been replaced with housing developments and shopping centers.

I parked in the garage at the rear of the hospital property and walked to the emergency room. The triage nurse at the front desk directed me to the curtained area where I found Rick propped up on a gurney. He wore a pale green gown in place of his shirt, and I could see leads attached to a heart monitor, and a regular up-and-down display on the monitor beside him.

"How are you feeling?"

"Better. As soon as I told the doctor what my job is, she decided it was some kind of stress-related thing. And I didn't even get to tell her about the unsolved homicides."

"Don't worry about them. Focus on keeping your heart rate steady. When they let you out, you should call Tamsen. Take the day off and stay home with Rascal. Petting Rochester and playing with him always calms me down when I'm stressed."

"Not sure the chief of police will see it that way."

I sat on the stool beside his bed. "Things are slow at Friar Lake, so I've got some flexible time. Anything I can do to help you out?"

"Ask Rochester for a clue? Or use your online mojo to find me a murderer?"

"Working on it." I told him about looking through Joel Goldberg's emails and online posts. "There's a guy I want to track down. He's got a weird screen name, Not Who I Think I Am, and Joel's been emailing him about Holocaust survivors in Trenton."

The doctor returned then, a young Chinese woman who barely looked old enough for college. Her name tag indicated she was Dr. Chen, and she had a California surfer lilt to her voice.

I stood back as she scanned through Rick's chart and then glanced at the monitor. "Your signs are all stable," she said. "I can write you a prescription for an SSRI to relieve some of your stress, but the best thing you can do is work out ways to relieve it yourself."

Rick nodded. "I know. Exercise. Play with the dog." "You're single?" she asked.

"He's almost engaged," I said. "About to propose."

"Are you experiencing stress from that situation?" she asked Rick.

He pursed his lips for a moment. "In a way. Not about the proposal, you know. I'm sure I want to marry Tamsen. Just making the time to do it right."

"This is a good reason to spend some time with your almost-fiancée. Kissing and cuddling are great stress relievers."

She electronically prescribed a medication for him. "I'll have the nurse come in and disconnect you, and then you're good to go." She wagged a finger at him. "I don't want to see you back here, Mr. Stemper. You take care of yourself."

She left with a swish of her white coat. "Have you called Tamsen yet?" I asked.

"I don't want to worry her. Don't want her to think I'm some sick old guy she's going to have to take care of."

"I doubt she'll think that. And I'm sure she'd want to know you're here."

He looked at his watch. "Justin left for school a half hour ago, so she's probably sitting at her kitchen table with a cup of coffee, reading email on her phone."

I liked the way Rick was already so familiar with Tamsen's schedule. "Then call her. I'll wait out in the lobby for you to finish up and then I'll drive you home."

While I waited for Rick, I checked my college email on my phone. What did we do before we were so tethered? I was able to answer a couple of messages without even opening a computer.

"I spoke to Tam," Rick said, when he walked out of the ER door. "You were right, she expected me to call her instead of you. She's going to come over later and check in on me."

"Good. Be sure to get in some of that stress relief the doctor was talking about."

As we drove back to Stewart's Crossing I told Rick what I'd learned from Saul Benesch. "I think he knows something more than he's telling," I said. "I can't say how—just a feeling."

"Maybe I should give Mr. Benesch a call," Rick said.

"No, hold off for a day or so. Let me work on him first. There is someone you ought to talk to, though." I told him about the young woman with the Medusa hair that Gail had mentioned the night before. "Gail was worried she might be trying to take advantage of Daniel Epstein."

"Great. Racial profiling?"

"I don't think the girl's race matters. The way Gail described seeing them together made her uneasy. That's all."

"I'll give her a call. Epstein's son gave me his father's phone records so maybe I can match her up to someone he was in contact with recently."

I dropped Rick at his house and retrieved Rochester, and then drove up River Road to Friar Lake. The willows along the river had lost most of their leaves, and I could see the water between the barren branches. Winter was coming.

And I had some hacking to do.

Chapter 25
What's in a Name

After a cursory glance at incoming emails and my own to-do list, I knuckled down to make a plan. What did I know, and what did I want to know?

First on my list was the mysterious person Joel Goldberg had been emailing with, NotwhoIthinkIam. Who indeed?

I started surfing through a list of genealogy websites, hoping that Notwho had used the same handle in various sites. I found that he'd posted on several threads. The most interesting concerned people who had changed their names after the Holocaust.

Some had changed for pragmatic reasons – difficulty in spelling, or a desire not to wear their Jewish name in a world that had proved hostile to their people. Others had patriotic reasons – film producer Menahem Golan had changed his surname from Globus in honor of the Golan Heights. Others had changed as a way to start over again in a new place, leaving their old identity behind.

NotWho had asked Joel if he knew anything about someone named Karl Kurtz, and Joel hadn't been able to find anything. But I had a few more tricks up my sleeve than Joel did. My fingers tingled with the thrill of hacking as flexed them, then hunted through my hard drive for a program that could break into a poorly-guarded database.

I was doing exactly what had sent me to prison in the first place—breaking into places I didn't belong in service of what I believed was a greater good. I hoped that I'd learned a few things since then—how to hide my tracks better, for example. And this time I was determined that I would take down this killer before anyone else died.

Once I had the program initiated, I entered the addresses for several databases and told the program to search for both Kurtz and Feinberg, then pop up a message with the results.

While that worked in the background, I went to one of the forums where NotWho had participated. With a couple of keystrokes, I was able to view the information the user had provided when setting up the ID. I was stunned to find that the email address used belonged to Saul Benesch.

Was that what Benesch was hiding? That he wasn't who he thought he was? And what did that mean, anyway?

I needed to talk to Benesch again, but I didn't know him well enough to call him or drop in on him. I didn't even have the connection that I had with Henry Namias, who had known my mother. I'd have to wait until the Talmud study group on Wednesday.

Suddenly my laptop pinged with an incoming alert from the website where I'd left the query about Kurtz earlier. The name Karl Kurtz had been found in a database for a displaced persons camp called Feldafing, near Munich, in what was in those immediate postwar years the American zone of occupation.

The record was skimpy. Kurtz said that he was a Jew aged twenty-two, a native of Berlin, and that he had been living underground under an assumed name. He wanted to emigrate to the United States.

That was it. No record of whatever happened to him.

When I looked up, Rochester was on the floor with the translation between his paws. "That does not belong to you," I said, pulling it away from him. Fortunately he hadn't chewed it, though there was a big drop of drool on the page, nearly covering the name Kalman Feinberg.

Why did that name resonate with me? I read through the document carefully. Aaron Feinberg had died at Auschwitz soon after he, his brother and Hafetz had been locked up there, but Kalman and Hafetz had been put to work.

My brain finally made the connection. Aaron Feinberg was the president of Shomrei Torah. Was he descended from Aaron and Kalman Feinberg?

But he couldn't be. According to Hafetz, Kalman had died at Auschwitz about six months before the camp was liberated. I remembered the photo I'd found that included my mother, the one from a speech by a Holocaust survivor named Kalman Feinberg.

Had to be a different man. Feinberg was a common Jewish name, as was Aaron. Kalman was less familiar to me, but perhaps it had been popular in Berlin at the time. I had certainly seen certain names recurring in my classes at Eastern – Jessica, Kyle, Justin and so on.

The Feldafing database was still open on my laptop, and on a whim I typed in the name Kalman Feinberg. I was stunned to see a result, a form filled out when someone left the camp.

Kalman Feinberg, a Jew aged twenty-three and native of Berlin, had been granted a visa to emigrate to the United States. The Hebrew Immigrant Aid Society had found a place for him to live and a job.

In Trenton, New Jersey.

My brain buzzed with connections. This was the man, then, who had spoken to the youth group my mother belonged to about his experience during the Holocaust. The father of Aaron Feinberg, president of Shomrei Torah. He had been in Feldafing at the same time as this mysterious Karl Kurtz. Did they know each other? They were the same age, both Jews from Berlin.

Could Myer Hafetz have been mistaken, and Aaron Feinberg survived? Perhaps he'd simply been transferred to another camp, and Hafetz had lost track of him.

I went back through the database looking for an entry form for Feinberg, but couldn't find one.

I looked at Rochester. "Kurtz went into the camp but never left.

Feinberg never entered the camp, but left it."

He looked up at me, then rolled back on his side. "Don't you see it, puppy? Maybe Kurtz and Feinberg are the same person. And Kurtz was German, not Jewish."

He yawned.

Was his disinterest because I was on the wrong track? Or just that he wanted to take a nap?

When he entered the camp, Kurtz admitted that he had been living under a different name in hiding. Perhaps during his stay he had merely reappropriated his own name? Or like many others, he'd chosen a new name to go with his new life. Nothing illegal or immoral about that.

I had too many ideas buzzing in my brain and I needed to talk to Rick. How was I going to tell him that I'd gotten this information? Should I be honest? After all, he'd asked me to work my online mojo. He knew that meant hacking, didn't he? Or was he so certain that I was following a straight and narrow path that he hadn't warned me to be honest?

I left Friar Lake early and headed to Rick's house. "I'm fine," he protested, as he opened the door. "Tam was here for a few hours. She cleaned up and made me dinner to heat up later."

Rochester romped past me to play with Rascal, and I followed Rick into the living room. "I'm glad you're better because I need to talk to you," I said.

By then I had decided I'd tell Rick how I had searched the databases, without mentioning that I'd had to break in. If he asked, I'd be honest. But I didn't want us to get sidetracked in a discussion of my problems if I didn't have to.

I laid out the situation between Kurtz and Feinberg. "One man comes into the camp, another goes out," I said.

"Wasn't one of them the guy in that document you had translated?" he asked.

I pulled it out of my messenger bag. The spot of drool Rochester had left on Kalman Feinberg's name was dry but still discolored. I handed the paper to Rick.

"See here?" he said, after he'd read for a moment. "This guy Hafetz says that Kalman Feinberg died at Auschwitz. So how did he end up at this Feldafing place?"

I looked at the paper with him.

"Hold on," I said after a minute. "Suppose Kurtz was lying about being Jewish when he entered the camp. I read about it, and it was the first all-Jewish displaced persons camp set up. Once you got in there, you had a golden ticket to go to Israel or the United States."

"So Kurtz pretended to be Jewish to get in," Rick said. "But isn't there a basic problem with pretending something like that?"

"What do you mean?"

He pointed to the place in Hafetz's testimony where the police had forced him to drop his pants. "Wouldn't they check that in the camp?"

"You mean to see if he was circumcised?" I turned to my laptop. "Hold on a minute."

I did a quick search, then turned the screen so Rick could read. "This says that some German Jews didn't circumcise their sons because they wanted to be modern. He could have said that."

"OK. So this Kurtz, a German, not Jewish, shows up at the camp and convinces them to let him in so that he can take advantage of the immigration options."

"And he changes his name to someone he knew back in Berlin who died. Maybe to honor his memory or hide his background. Maybe just because it was easier."

"And he comes to Trenton as Kalman Feinberg. Then what?" Rick asked.

"He gets a job, he gets married. And Myer Hafetz shows up." "Who was also from Berlin, and knew that the real Kalman

Feinberg died at Auschwitz." Rick nodded. "But why does that matter to Kurtz-slash-Feinberg?"

"Because he lied," I said. "He married a Jewish woman. He named his son after the dead man's brother. In the two years before Hafetz arrived, he had become a big shot at Shomrei Torah."

"It's a big step from that to killing someone – to killing two people," Rick said. "And right now this is all just conjecture. We could be totally on the wrong track."

"I need to talk to Saul Benesch," I said. "He might have the key here. Why was he looking for Karl Kurtz now?" I told Rick about my plan to speak with Benesch at the Talmud study group on Wednesday morning.

"Be careful what you say," Rick said. "You don't want to be the next one in this killer's crosshairs."

Chapter 26
Everything Lost

The dogs were still having fun and Rochester resisted my call to get him to leave. Twice. The third time I walked up to him and grabbed a hank of fur from the back of his neck. "March, mister," I said. He looked up at me with those soulful big brown eyes, like I was destroying all chance of him having happiness in this world.

I relented, as I almost always do. "Fine. You can have five more minutes of play."

I released my grip on him, and he immediately went down on his front paws in the play posture. Rascal yipped, and then they took off.

"Puppy whipped," Rick said. Then he held up his hand. "And before you say anything, I know, I'm just as bad as you are."

Five minutes turned into ten, as Rick and I sat and talked about nothing in particular. When Rochester was momentarily tired out, he and I left.

When I got home, Lili wanted to know about Rick. "He seems to be okay, but he's got to take some pills for stress."

"He's got to ask Tamsen to marry him," Lili said. "She'll take care of him."

It was funny – I'd thought Rick and Tamsen were a good match, because he had a caretaker personality, and as a young widow with a son, she needed someone to take care of her. But she was a strong, independent woman, accustomed to being a mother, and I realized that they could take care of each other.

Lili and I were each other's best friend, backup and sounding board, and I knew first-hand that the stress relief Dr. Chen had prescribed for Rick was very therapeutic.

Sadly, Lili was still catching up on all the work she'd missed while she was in Florida, so there was no kissing or cuddling for us. Instead she went up to the office to grade papers online, and I stayed downstairs with Rochester.

Lili was pragmatic about my hacking. She understood that I had a compulsion to sneak into places online where I shouldn't be, that I was trying my best to control behavior that might get me sent back to prison. So I did my best not to do things in front of her that might upset her or provoke an argument.

With her safely upstairs, though, I could I turn on the laptop that contained my hacking tools. As I did, I thought about the conclusions I'd come to. How could I verify that Karl Kurtz, who entered Feldafing camp, was the same man as Kalman Feinberg, who left it? There was no exit record for Kurtz, or entry record for Feinberg, but that was just the starting point for a hypothesis.

I went back to the results of the database program I had set up to search for Kurtz and Feinberg. I'd stopped paying attention to it when I discovered the reference to Kurtz at Feldafing, but now I check the full results, which had been saved in a text file on the laptop's hard drive.

There were no more records of the Karl Kurtz who had been born in 1922 in Berlin after his entry into the Feldafing camp. I did find a couple of places that had mentioned someone by his name as one of the guards at Auschwitz, but I dismissed those, because the Kurtz I was looking for was Jewish, and I'd already established that the name Kurtz could be used by Jews and non-Jews alike—as long as they had a short ancestor.

The Kalman Feinberg who had been born in Berlin that same

year had a much fuller life story. He had been recorded as entering Auschwitz, though his name was not among those on any list of prisoners freed.

I looked at Rochester. "What do you think, boy?" I asked. "Did Feinberg slip through the cracks? Maybe his record is here, but his name was misspelled."

Rochester woofed and shook his head.

"No? Then you think he died in the concentration camp?"

He woofed again, louder, and this time he went down on his front paws in the play posture. I got up and fetched him a treat from the box in the kitchen, and he sat beside me crunching noisily.

I looked back at the screen and the name Auschwitz jumped out at me. I couldn't hear or say that name without a bit of a shudder, and a thank you to the Lord who had thus far kept me from suffering that kind of horror.

Auschwitz. Auschwitz.

I went back to the records on Kurtz and looked at the statements by survivors that said he had been a guard there. Suppose that was true, and that after the war was over Kurtz had appropriated Feinberg's identity. They were the same age, after all, both from Berlin. How hard would it have been during that chaotic time after the camps were liberated to step up and pretend to be someone else?

Someone whose whole family was dead. Who was left to know of the deception? He had known Feinberg as a boy, knew that Feinberg's whole family had been killed.

The answer came to me in flash that felt almost like the onset of a headache.

Myer Hafetz knew. He had known both Feinbergs in Berlin and seen both die at Auschwitz. Then he had the bad luck to be sent to Trenton, New Jersey, where a man was pretending to be his old friend.

A man who had been a guard at the very camp where his friend had died.

What would Hafetz do if he discovered Kurtz masquerading as

Feinberg? Write up the testimony for Yad Vashem? Then use that paper to confront Kurtz?

Kurtz had already started a new life by then. I checked the records and discovered that he had married by then, a woman named Hina Levine, and begun working in the furniture store owned by his father-in-law.

I knew that eventually Hina's father would die, that Kalman would inherit the company and rename it Feinberg's Fine Furniture, that he would become president of Shomrei Torah.

But back then, he was a young man with a terrible past that anyone would want to forget, and a bright future ahead of him. If Hafetz told the community who he really was, he might be arrested for his role in the camp. Tried, sentenced, deported. Divorced.

Everything lost. If only there was some way to keep Hafetz quiet.

Kurtz had found that way. But what if before he died, Hafetz had confided in Rabbi Sapinsky? That was very believable – who else would Hafetz be able to confide in?

With Hafetz dead, the rabbi might have spoken with Kurtz himself—which triggered his death. Because of the tensions between immigrants and natives, it was logical to me that the rabbi would have tried to solve the problem within his community, rather than involve the police.

But that didn't explain why someone had killed Joel Goldberg, or Daniel Epstein. Kalman Feinberg – or Karl Kurtz – was long dead, and beyond any earthly punishment.

Unless I was wrong about something. I went back to the mysterious online individual who billed himself NotwhoIthinkIam, and had used Saul Benesch's email address. What was Benesch's connection to this whole business?

He had been a boy in Trenton at the time of the two deaths, and I found it hard to believe he was guilty of them. Could he have discovered somehow that his father was not the man he believed, but Karl Kurtz instead?

That would explain the online moniker. But why commit murder over it?

"I am so glad to be caught up," Lili said, from the top of the stairs, and I quickly shut down the laptop.

"Congratulations," I called up to her.

"Are you going to come up here and celebrate with me, or are you going to stay down there?"

The answer to that was clear.

Chapter 27
Urban Myth

Tuesday morning I left a message for Rick. I wanted to talk over my suspicions with him, but he hadn't called me back by the time I had to leave Friar Lake for the Jewish Lit class.

I dropped Rochester at Lili's office, and kicked off the discussion in class by mentioning my search into name origins. "That made me think about how our names are such an integral part of our identity. How does having a name that identifies us as part of a religion or an ethnicity make us think about ourselves?"

"My uncle changed his name from Plotnick to Platt when my cousins were little," Noah said. "He said he didn't want his kids to be discriminated against."

"My father's family is Italian," Ryan Giordano said. "Sometimes it's weird for me, having an Italian name but being Jewish."

A young black woman named Shonda Levy said, "My great-great-grandfather was a Portuguese Jew who married a Jamaican woman, and nobody in my family is Jewish. But people always assume that my father's a white guy, or that somehow my family converted."

I didn't want to tell her that in Yiddish a "shonda" was a sin, so it was unlikely a Jewish child would ever have been given that name. But Noah didn't have the same inhibition and he blurted it out.

I had to quickly change the subject, reading out from a website I'd found, which indicated that while some German-speaking Jews took last names as early as the 17th century, most Ashkenazi Jews were among the last Europeans to take family names. They were accustomed to the patronymic – son of, daughter of, and didn't change until they were forced to, first in the Austro-Hungarian Empire in 1787 and then in Czarist Russia in 1844.

"There are people whose names were changed when they immigrated," Jessica said.

"That's an urban myth," Noah said. I wanted to disagree with him, because I remembered an incident I knew of when an American draft-dodger went to Canada—his last name had been misspelled on his paperwork, and he'd adopted that new name.

Instead, I pulled up a website which agreed with Noah, and that led us to all kinds of other reasons why people changed their names. To avoid the law, because their gender changed, or because they didn't like the name they'd been stuck with at birth.

We segued into the names of characters in the works we'd read, as well as their authors. As students called out names, I put a list on the board, and then I assigned them to do some research on their phones and laptops and then make brief presentations. The diversity of names on the board was fascinating, from Emma Lazarus and her connection to the dead man Jesus had risen from the grave, to the expected Biblical references like Abraham Cahan, to all the names that ended in –stein, -ski and so on.

By the end of class I had tied it all back to the questions of identity that Jewish American authors explored. I used names as well as Jewish stereotypes like big noses or greedy behavior, which went all the way back to Shakespeare's Shylock and before that.

When I stopped at Lili's office to retrieve Rochester, Lili was standing by her secretary's desk. "How's your class going?" she asked.

"It's interesting. We talk a lot about identity, what it means to be a Jew, or an American. It's so relevant to what's going on in the world today."

"I agree. I have a girl from Syria in my introduction to photography class and she has a great eye, and a real aptitude for the technical aspects, too. If her family hadn't had the opportunity to come to this country she'd have no chance at an education."

I told Lili I'd see her at home and attached Rochester's leash to his collar, and we walked back to where I'd parked. On the way I checked my phone and realized that Rick had finally returned my call. Instead of calling him back, though, I drove directly to the Stewart's Crossing Police Station.

The desk sergeant there was an old friend of Rochester's, and usually slipped him one of the biscuits he kept in his desk for the K-9 officers. The big golden settled behind the desk as the sergeant called Rick. "You can go on in," he said to me, and I walked past the bullpen to the small office Rick used.

"She said yes!" Rick crowed when I stepped in the office. We fist-bumped.

"I expected she would. Did she like the ring?"

"She loved it. She said it's just what she would have picked out herself. And she was impressed that I knew her birthstone." He sat down in his chair and I sat across from him.

"At least that's one good thing going on," he continued. "You know the mayor lives in Crossing Estates, don't you? Only a couple of blocks from Daniel Epstein's house. He's called the police chief a half dozen times, stressing about somebody breaking into a neighbor's house and killing him."

"You said it wasn't a break-in," I reminded Rick. "That Epstein let his killer in."

"Semantics," Rick said. He groaned. "Jesus, I'm starting to talk like you. Worrying about grammar and word choice."

"That must be a sign you're feeling better. If you're emulating me."

"So what brings you down here?"

"I have a theory I want to run past you." I explained the idea that concentration camp guard Karl Kurtz had usurped the identity of a dead neighbor after the war.

"What proof do you have?"

"It's not so much proof as absence of proof," I said, and Rick groaned. I went through all the steps I'd taken to establish what had happened to both Kalman Feinberg and Karl Kurtz after the war. That work had been legit, which I made a point of mentioning. "Kurtz drops off the radar," I said.

"If he really was a concentration camp guard, there's a good reason for that," Rick said. "He could have gone underground in Germany. Why go to the trouble of claiming someone else's identity?"

"Because he wanted to come to the United States? It was still hard to emigrate here from Germany, and only the Jews got preferential treatment and help from aid agencies."

"The pieces fit together," Rick admitted. "But we're still not seeing the whole outline of the puzzle." He leaned back in his chair. "I was able to track down the woman with the hair that Gail mentioned. We found some fingerprints in Mr. Epstein's house, and one of them led us to her. Her name is Shenita Durban and she says that Epstein was mentoring her as she tried to start a business. She said that she went over to Epstein's house once so he could give her some books."

"But her fingerprints were on file?"

"She was arrested a couple of years ago for petty larceny," Rick said. "She put all the blame on her boyfriend and she got off with some hours of community service." He sat back. "The boyfriend's a different story, though. We didn't find his prints at the house, but he has a record for breaking and entering."

"But if this woman is involved, that would mean that Joel Goldberg's death is not connected to Daniel Epstein's. And that doesn't make sense to me."

"Sense or not, I have to follow every lead. When are you going to talk to that other guy, Benesch?"

"Tomorrow morning after Talmud study," I said. "I want to ask him if that online ID belongs to him, and see where the conversation goes after that. I still don't see what connection he has to Kurtz."

"If you find out anything – anything at all – I want you to call me right away. Don't go off in your usual half-assed way."

"Thanks for the vote of confidence," I said. "But I agree. I'm not interested in chasing any more killers, thank you very much."

I retrieved Rochester from the sergeant's desk and we drove home, where Lili was already in the kitchen sautéing chicken breasts. I kissed her hello. "She said yes."

"That's great! Keep an eye on these breasts and turn them over before they burn. I'm going to call Rick."

I heard her side of the conversation as I studied the chicken. How I would I know when they were about to burn? Why not just turn them over now and avoid a problem?

"The football field?" I heard her say. "What possessed you to propose to her there?"

I knew why. Rick had met Tamsen when he coached her son's Pop Warner football team. It seemed like a perfectly reasonable guy choice to make—it was romantic, because of their history there, and also because it brought her son Justin into the picture, too.

I lifted one corner of a breast up and peered at it. Looked pretty done to me. So I flipped both of them, with a satisfying sizzle as the raw meat hit the hot surface.

Lili returned to the kitchen and took over, and my mind drifted back to the conversation we'd had in class about names, and then how Henry Namias had remembered my mother when I gave her maiden name.

"Do you think Tamsen will change her name?" I asked Lili.

"I doubt it. She's already established in her career, and she has a son by that name. I doubt Rick would mind. Would you?"

I shook my head. "These days it seems weird to me when a

woman takes her husband's name after marriage, the way Tamsen did. Every now and then I'll be in some female faculty member's office and see her diploma on the wall and realize that's her maiden name. I wonder if it's different when she's coming into the marriage with another man's last name."

"I never changed mine," Lili said. "Thank god. At the time I didn't want to bother with the paperwork. Now I'm grateful. If I'd started my career under either Philip's or Adriano's last name I'm not sure what I'd do." She smiled. "Although my mother could never figure out why I didn't. 'You aren't a real wife unless you take his name,' she said, more than one time." She shrugged. "I guess she was right, and I never was a real wife."

I was able to avoid that minefield because the breasts were done, and I had to help Lili serve them up over a bed of wild rice. As we ate, I asked, "How is your mother doing?"

"She's in therapy every morning. They have her up and moving around with a walker. She hates it, of course, but I keep reminding her that the quicker she gets better, the quicker she can go back to her apartment."

"Is she going back there? Or to Fed's?"

"I don't know. If we can get an aide to stay with her, maybe she can stay in the apartment for a while longer. She doesn't want to move in with Fedi and Sara, and I'm pretty sure Sara doesn't want that either."

I understood Sara's position, while at the same time I hoped that if her mother-in-law had to come live with them, she'd adjust. I'd never met the woman myself, but I knew from long experience what Jewish women were like. I remembered that Victor Namias had called his wife a *balabusta*, and I was pretty sure both Lili and Sara fit that category as well.

The next morning, I took Rochester for a quick walk before I had to leave for Shomrei Torah. As we stopped and started around River Bend, I thought about names and what they said about us. My own name, Levitan, came from the Polish for Jew—Levite, plus a Slavic suffix of -an. Couldn't get more Jewish than that.

The most famous person I'd found with my name was a Russian landscape painter named Isaac Levitan, who had been born in Lithuania, where my ancestors had lived, though I had no idea if he was related to me. My mother's maiden name, Gordon, was even more common, deriving, I believed, from the city of Grodno in modern-day Belarus. And of course there were tons of non-Jewish Gordons coming from England, Scotland and other countries.

Rochester and I were among the first to arrive at Talmud study, and Rabbi Goldberg pulled me aside to asked if I'd made any progress in figuring out what had happened to Joel. I had to admit that I still had more questions than answers, but that I hoped to know more soon.

I didn't pay much attention to the conversation among the group, thinking about how I was going to approach Saul Benesch. I made sure to walk out with him, and as soon as we were away from the building, I said, "It's so sad about Daniel Epstein. I can't stop thinking about him. But at least he had a good sense of who he was, and where he belonged in the community."

"That's true," Benesch said. "We old-timers, we have deep roots here. I wish my children hadn't moved away, that my grandchildren could grow up here, where our family history is, and all around each other."

"So you really know who you are," I said. "I do."

"Then why did you use the online ID NotwhoIthinkIam?" I asked.

He looked at me curiously. "I have no idea what you're talking about."

"You haven't been searching through online databases for information about Holocaust survivors?"

"Sonny, you've got the wrong guy. The only thing I do on the computer is send emails and look at pictures of my grandchildren on

Facebook. I'm so computer illiterate that Aaron had to come over and set everything up for me."

The wheels started turning in my head. "So Aaron Feinberg knows your email ID and password?"

Benesch appeared to have figured out what was going on, because he looked around furtively. "I can't talk here."

"I'll buy you a cup of coffee at the Chocolate Ear," I said. "I can take Rochester inside there. I have some information you need to hear."

"I'm afraid of that," Benesch said, but he agreed to meet me.

Chapter 28
Three Shots

On the way to the Chocolate Ear, I kept going back to NotwhoIthinkIam. If Aaron Feinberg knew Benesch's ID and password, he could have used them to shield his identity for his online searching.

What was he looking for, though? Was his father really Karl Kurtz? Why would he look online for verification otherwise?

I got to the café before Benesch, and parked Rochester in the doggy annex. Then I met Benesch at the counter in the café. "What can I get for you?" I asked, as I pulled out my credit card.

"Just a small coffee." I ordered a grande mocha for myself and the coffee for him, and we stepped aside to wait.

"All these fancy coffee drinks," Benesch said. "Seems silly to me. Your generation, you're so spoiled. You want everything the way you want it."

"And if we can afford it, why not?" I asked. "It must have been tough growing up in Trenton during the war years and afterwards."

"I saw a man be murdered," Benesch said abruptly. "I never told anyone because I was too scared."

My heart skipped a couple of beats. Gail's assistant handed us our coffees and I handed Benesch his. "I'd like to hear about that, if you feel like you can tell me."

"It's time," he said. He followed me into the annex and we sat down at a table, with Rochester on the floor beside me.

"I wasn't a very good Torah student," he said after a moment or two. "All I wanted to do was play sports. Baseball, football, stickball. For my bar mitzvah, I had to study extra hours with Rabbi Sapinsky."

His eyes clouded over, as if he was remembering those days.

"I used to have to go over there after school was out. But one day I joined a ball game and I was late. I got to the shul and went looking for the rabbi. I heard him arguing with someone and then a noise."

He stopped for a moment.

"What kind of noise?" I asked gently.

"Today I'd probably recognize it as a gunshot, but back then all I knew was that it was like the sound the bat makes when you hit the ball with it." He took a deep breath. "And then a man came running past me. He didn't see me, because I was in the corner. I didn't recognize him but I was worried about the rabbi so I went back the way he'd come. I found the rabbi on the floor of his office, blood pouring out of his head."

Benesch began to shiver. "I was so scared, I didn't know what to do. I rushed home and told my mother, and she went to the shul. When she came home she asked me, Solly, do you know what happened to the rabbi?"

Of course. Saul, Solly. Saul Benesch was the boy mentioned in the police reports. I pulled out my cell phone while Benesch was lost in his memory and texted Rick, asking him to come to the Chocolate Ear ASAP. If he didn't arrive to speak with Benesch himself, I'd have to make sure he heard Benesch's story at some point.

"I didn't want to admit that I'd been playing ball when I should have been studying, and I was too scared that the man would come after me if I told anyone I had seen him. So I said nothing."

Then he looked up at me. "It wasn't until years later, when my wife and I joined Shomrei Torah, that I recognized the man I saw running away from the rabbi." He took a deep breath. "It was Kalman Feinberg, Aaron's father."

"Have you ever told anyone else?"

He shook his head. "Who can I tell? Aaron is my friend, and he idolized his father. It would destroy him if he learned something like this."

I had a feeling that Aaron had learned a lot more about his father.

"Did you know a man named Myer Hafetz?" I asked. "He was a cousin of Henry Namias's family."

"No. What about him?"

"I think Kalman Feinberg killed him, too."

I explained my theory. "I think Aaron Feinberg's father was really a German man named Karl Kurtz, who had been a guard at Auschwitz. After the real Kalman Feinberg died, Kurtz assumed his identity and came to the United States to start over. Then he ran into Myer Hafetz, who recognized him, and he killed Hafetz, and then the rabbi, to protect himself."

I looked up and saw Rick walk into the café, and motioned him over. As he petted Rochester hello, I introduced the two of them. "Mr. Benesch, would you tell Detective Stemper what you told me?"

He nodded. "Yes, it's time."

I stood up and Rick took my seat. I caught his eye and he nodded slightly.

As I drove up to Friar Lake with Rochester by my side, I talked out my ideas with him. "Aaron Feinberg must be the man behind NotwhoIthinkIam," I said. "He helped Benesch set up his email account so he knew the ID and password, and he could use it hide his own identity on line."

Rochester didn't argue, so I continued.

"He must have gotten suspicious about his father's identity at some point and started looking for information. But that's all in the past. Why would it matter now?"

I stuck my hand out to stroke Rochester's head, but instead he sat up and licked my fingers. I laughed. "You are such a love bug." He yawned, and settled back in his seat.

Love. I'd loved my father, to the point of idolizing him when I was young, something I was sure a lot of boys felt. How would my love for my father change if I found out he'd been lying to me all my life? Would I be sad? Angry? Take that anger out on others?

It was his father's secret – but it was his, too, wasn't it? Suppose everyone in Trenton knew that Aaron Feinberg, big *macher* at Shomrei Torah and owner of several prosperous furniture stores in the suburbs, was the son of a concentration camp guard rather than a Holocaust survivor?

It would be an explosive story that would ruin his family. He'd have to give up being temple president. It would be too much of a slap in the face of the congregation for him to continue. And he'd probably have to sell or shut down his business—who would want to buy from someone with his background?

By the time we reached the office I felt sure that Aaron Feinberg had been behind the murders of Joel Goldberg and Daniel Epstein. I understood why he'd want to protect his secret, but I still couldn't figure out what had set him on a collision course with his two victims.

It was late that afternoon when my phone rang with an unknown number. "Steve? Aaron Feinberg here. Saul told me you've been talking to him."

I was stunned that Saul Benesch would have called Feinberg, after all we'd discussed. Wasn't he worried about his own life? And how did I know that Feinberg hadn't killed Benesch after that conversation?

I decided to play dumb. "I have."

"Saul's pretty upset about my using his email address and I'd like to explain the situation to you. Then maybe you can help me calm Saul down."

I hoped that meant Benesch was still alive.

I doubted that there was anything Feinberg could say that would explain away everything that had happened, but I said, "Sure. When did you want to get together?"

"We have a board meeting at Shomrei Torah tonight that I can't get out of. You live in River Bend, don't you? I have a friend who lives over there so I know it's not too far from the temple. Maybe you could swing by when the meeting is over and we can talk? But don't bring your dog, please. Take him for a walk before you leave."

Was that how he'd lured Joel Goldberg to his death, by arranging a meeting at Shomrei Torah? Hey, if it worked once. Only I'd make sure that Rick was there to look out for me.

I agreed to meet him outside the rabbi's study at nine o'clock that evening.

Then I called Rick and explained the situation. "You'll go with me, won't you?" I asked.

"Or I could just pull Mr. Feinberg in for questioning and leave you out of it."

"What are you going to question him about? You don't have any evidence connecting him to either murder, do you? Everything we know is just supposition."

"I am a skilled investigator, remember? I do this for a living. I ask people questions and get answers."

I waited.

"But you're right," he said eventually. "I can ask him all the questions I want but there's no guarantee he'll say anything that incriminates him."

We arranged that he'd pick me up at eight so that he could be in place to observe my meeting with Feinberg. "Do you want me to wear a wire?" I asked.

He said he'd take care of everything, and as I drove home I thought about questions that I'd want to ask Aaron Feinberg. How could I ease my way into asking him about his father? I doubted that he'd admit he'd killed Joel or Daniel, but I wanted to get enough information so that Rick would have the ability to pull him in for interrogation.

As we were driving into River Bend, I got a text from Lili that she had to stick around campus to meet with an adjunct who taught a night class, and that she'd be home late. When I stopped the car in my driveway, I texted her back a couple of kisses.

"Looks like it's just you and me, boy," I said. I ate dinner, fed the hound, and then took him for a long walk, still trying to put together the questions I wanted to ask Feinberg. I was so caught up those thoughts that I didn't worry too much about meeting with someone who might have killed twice already—I was younger than Feinberg, stronger, aware of what I was walking into, unlike Joel Goldberg or Daniel Epstein.

And I'd have Rick watching my back.

It was a cool night and I was glad to get back home. Rick arrived around eight and parked his truck beside my car. When I opened the door to him, Rochester kept nosing around, wondering why Rascal wasn't with him.

"Take off your shirt so I can hook up the wire," Rick said. I did as asked, and he taped a wire to my chest. "Sorry, this is going to hurt when it comes off. Unless you want to shave your chest."

"I'll suffer for justice."

The recorder went into my pants pocket, and then I put my shirt on. Rick opened a big bag and pulled out a black vest.

"Is that what I think it is?"

"Finest Kevlar," he said. "Stops a bullet up to a .44 magnum. I borrowed it for you from one of the other guys."

The vest looked bulky, with a front panel made of something shiny with a cross-hatched pattern across the front.

"You think I need this?"

"If we're correct, this guy has already shot and killed two men. I don't want my best friend to be the third."

Aw, that was sweet. It was also kind of scary. I was glad I was leaving Rochester behind. I slipped the vest on, and Rick tightened the straps on the vest. For a moment I had trouble breathing. "Too tight?" he asked.

"Yes," I gasped.

He loosened it a bit, then I put my windbreaker on over it. "Looks good," he said. "Let's hope he doesn't try for a head shot."

"I don't know about this, Rick," I said. "Maybe you're right, you should just pull him in for questioning."

"You know I don't have enough evidence for that."

I looked at myself in the mirror. I looked bigger, tougher. Maybe that was just the vest, but I felt more confident. "I should take Rochester out for a quick pee before we go."

"I'll stay here. I have a couple of phone calls to make."

I put on Rochester's leash and we went outside. The streets of River Bend were narrow and there wasn't much guest parking, so it was difficult to navigate around parked cars. To our right, a car idled on the other side of the street, its headlights on, waiting for someone to come out of the house, so we turned left instead.

Rochester made a beeline for one of his favorite spots and lifted his leg. Behind me, I heard the car begin creeping forward, and I tugged Rochester's leash and stepped onto a neighbor's lawn to let the car pass.

"Come on," I said out loud. "Not you, boy. I hate it when cars go so slowly while we're waiting for them to pass." I turned around to look at the approaching headlights.

Everything happened so quickly that it was hard to figure out what was going on. I heard three quick pops, and at first I thought the car was backfiring. Rochester freaked at the sound and tugged me away from the street, toward the neighbor's house.

Then it felt like someone had punched me, hard, in the back.

Three times.

I tripped over a low hedge and went down, and Rochester began to bark.

Chapter 29
Dangerous Path

I heard a door bang open, and Rick yell, "Steve!"

"I'm okay," I called, though I wasn't sure I was. "Go after him!"

Rick jumped into his truck, turned the flashing light on, and zoomed down the street in pursuit of whoever had been driving that car. Rochester licked my face, and I petted him. "I'm okay, boy," I said, though my back hurt.

I gingerly stood up. What in the world had just happened?

It couldn't have been Aaron Feinberg in that car. He was supposed to be at a temple board meeting. Who else? Saul Benesch? Henry Namias? Someone I hadn't considered?

I was surprised none of my neighbors came out as I limped back toward the house with Rochester close beside me. Hadn't anyone heard the gunshots? It felt like I might have pulled a muscle in my leg when I fell. But if that was all that was wrong I was grateful.

A set of headlights approached, coming from the direction the car had gone. Was the shooter coming back to finish the job? I scrambled across the street, tugging Rochester behind me, and made it to the door as the headlights swung into the driveway.

Rochester barked and barked. "It's okay, puppy," I said, stroking his head. "It's just Mama Lili."

She hopped out of her car. "What's wrong with you? Why were you limping? And what are you wearing?"

I collapsed onto a kitchen chair. "It's a bulletproof vest. Hopefully it worked." "Steven."

It was rare to hear Lili use my full name, and the tone of voice she used did not bode well.

"Rick was here," I said. "He fitted me out with this vest, and a recorder, so I could go to Shomrei Torah tonight and meet with Aaron Feinberg. But someone took a couple of shots at me just now, and Rick went off after whoever it was."

"But you're all right?"

"I think so. Can you help me get my jacket and this vest off?" "Ai yi yi. What am I going to do with you? Stand up."

I stood, trying not to put pressure on the leg that felt strained. She slipped the windbreaker off and turned me around. "There are three bullet holes in this vest," she said, her voice shaking. "Oh, Steve. Sweetheart. Before I take this off I'm getting the first aid kit."

"I'm okay," I protested, but she hurried upstairs to the bathroom. I undid the front buckle on the vest but couldn't flex my arms enough to get it off.

When she returned, carrying a plastic box with a bunch of first aid supplies, she undid the straps. Then she took a deep breath and slipped the vest off me.

"Well, at least the vest did its job," she said. "Nothing got through."

I undid the buttons of my shirt and she took it off. "There's some redness and swelling on your back," she said. She pressed her finger into one of the spots.

"Ouch!"

"Good. Maybe if these hurt for a few days you'll think twice about putting yourself in danger again."

"It was going to be fine," I protested. "Rick was going to be right there with me."

She made a show of looking around the room, even under the table. "And where is Rick now? I don't see him."

"I told you, he went after whoever shot me."

"I think I preferred it when you were just hacking," she said. "At least you weren't in danger of getting killed."

"Just of going to prison," I said. She glared at me.

I held up my hands. "Sorry. You're right. But honestly, I didn't think I was in any danger, with this vest, and Rick right there for backup."

My phone trilled with the *Hawaii Five-O* ring tone. "You all right?" Rick asked when I answered.

"Yeah, I'm good. Three bullets in the vest, though."

"Hold on to them. I'm going to need them for ballistics. I chased that car through River Bend and saw the driver throw a weapon out the window. But he got stuck waiting for the gate to open to let him out."

"Who is it?"

"Aaron Feinberg. I'm waiting for a couple of uniforms to get here and take him in, and I'll go back and look for the gun."

I was angry at Feinberg and wanted to do something. "Tell me where you're going to look for the gun and I'll meet you there."

"I can manage. You rest up and I'll talk to you later. I'll need to get a full statement from you and get that vest back, but that can wait until tomorrow."

I hung up and looked at Lili. "You are never going to change, are you?" she asked.

I took a deep breath, and pain shot through my back. "I'm never going to stop trying."

"I guess that's all I can ask for," Lili said. "Let's go upstairs. There's some bruise cream I can rub on your back to reduce the swelling."

I didn't hear from Rick again until late that night, and that was only a text suggesting we meet at the Chocolate Ear the next morning. When Rochester and I got there, Rick was already sitting in the annex, with a café mocha for me and a biscuit for Rochester.

"There was no board meeting, you know," I said, as I sat down across from him. "I checked the Shomrei Torah website—the meeting's next Tuesday night."

"Might have been a good idea to check that earlier," Rick said dryly.

He had arrested Aaron Feinberg and spent a couple of hours questioning him. He hadn't admitted to killing anyone, but Rick had found the gun, a .38 millimeter Ruger semi-automatic, and which was registered to Feinberg.

I handed him the vest, and he looked at it, then whistled. "Not a bad shot for an old man," he said. "If you hadn't been wearing the vest these could have done some real damage."

"I was thinking about what Feinberg said to me when he asked me to meet. That he knew I lived in River Bend. That he suggested I take Rochester for a walk before I left for the temple."

"So that he could be in place to shoot you. A smart guy, though pretty twisted."

"What I don't understand is how Joel Goldberg made the connection to Feinberg. He couldn't have read that document in Yiddish that I found at the old shul."

"And see, he didn't have to," Rick said. "Feinberg told me that Joel was angry about the way he'd been treated when he showed up at the blessing of the animals. He had looked up Feinberg's address online and went to the house in Hiltonia to complain."

"The night that he died?"

Rick nodded. "He says that while he was there he showed Feinberg a paper he'd found hidden away at the old synagogue."

"It couldn't be what Myer Hafetz wrote. That was in Yiddish, and Joel couldn't read that. And I found it in the box behind the Belgian block wall."

"Apparently there was an English translation, and he brought that to Feinberg's house, and they went over it together. He says that he convinced Joel the document referred to someone else, and suggested that he turn it over to his brother. That Joel left, and that's the last he saw of him."

"Didn't the police pick up Joel in Hiltonia that night? Near Feinberg's house?"

"Yup. If I were a betting man I'd say that Joel left Feinberg's place, wandered around for a while, then went back to talk more. When Feinberg wouldn't open the door he got angry, and that's when a neighbor called the cops."

"So the police took Joel to the train station, and he got on the bus to Shomrei Torah," I said. "How did Feinberg know he was going there?"

"This is all conjecture, but I think maybe Joel said something like 'I'm going right over to the synagogue,' and so Feinberg went after him. He insists that he stayed at home that night, and his wife agrees he was there. Of course, I don't believe her."

"Did he admit to knowing about his father's background?"

"He told me he'd found some letters addressed to his father, calling him Karl. That he had done some looking around online, because he was curious. But he didn't know the whole story until he saw that document."

"Did he know that his father killed the rabbi and Myer Hafetz?"
"He swears he didn't. But he also says he didn't kill Joel Goldberg or Daniel Epstein."

"Why did he shoot at me, then?"

"He won't say. All he was willing to talk about was the past. Wouldn't say anything about Epstein, either, but I could tell he was lying from his body language. I'll leave the rest of the interrogation up to the district attorney. All I had to do was deliver probable cause, and I've done that."

We finished our coffees and Rick left. I walked Rochester back to the car but instead of heading up to Friar Lake, I detoured into Trenton. I drove past St. Francis Medical Center, where I was born, and then past where my grandmother and my great-aunts and uncles had lived.

Rochester sat up eagerly in the seat beside me. He didn't know where we were going – but then, neither did I. It wasn't until we passed the Rescue Mission and where the house with the two red doors had been that I realized I was heading for the old shul.

When we got there, a makeshift fence had been put up around the site and a construction crew was working on demolishing the last remnants of the building.

So much of my past was gone, I thought as I sat there in the car, petting Rochester. Every relative of my parents' generation. Many of the landmarks of my childhood and young adulthood. Trenton was a different city than the one where I'd spent so much time when I was a boy. Even Stewart's Crossing had changed in small ways. The feed store had been replaced by a real estate office. Stores and restaurants like Gail's café catered to a more upmarket clientele.

But despite all the changes, I still felt connected to the Delaware Valley, to the ghosts of old Jewtown. I would not have children to pass that connection on to, which was a shame, but perhaps some legacies needed to end—like Aaron Feinberg's.

Rochester and I watched the destruction of the last wall of the old shul, and then we drove quietly upriver to Friar Lake.

Friday night, Lili accompanied me to Shomrei Torah, where Rabbi Goldberg thanked me for all my help in establishing what Joel had wanted, and what had happened to him.

"Aaron Feinberg has resigned as temple president," he said. "He wouldn't tell me why, but Saul Benesch told me that Aaron was been arrested for Joel's murder and that he's out on bail now. Is that true?"

"I can't speak for the police, but I believe that's the case."

"And all for the sake of some old paperwork? That's why my brother died?"

The rabbi's pain was palpable.

"He was pursuing the truth," I said gently. "And we know that's always a dangerous path to take."

"When Joel would disappear for months on end, I'd have these nightmares where the police would contact me, that he was dead. Who knew he would die so close to me?"

Lili put her hand on the rabbi's arm. "What matters is that he came to you," she said. "Your bond as brothers was still strong right up to the end."

He smiled. "Yes, that's a comfort."

We left the synagogue a few minutes later. "There's something I've been meaning to ask you," Lili said as we walked to the car. A cold wind swept through the parking lot, shaking the dying leaves from the trees around us. "How would you feel about taking a trip to Florida at Christmas? We'll both have a couple of weeks off when the college is closed. We could drive down to Miami with Rochester and spend some time with my mother."

I thought of my own parents, and how much I wished I had time to spend with them again. "Of course," I said, and kissed her cheek, her skin cold, but warming at my touch.

Author's Note

Those who are familiar with Trenton's Jewish heritage may note that I've changed a few details to suit my plot. Shomrei Torah is obviously based on Har Sinai, the synagogue where my family belonged and where I was consecrated, attended Sunday and Hebrew school, celebrated my bar mitzvah, and was confirmed. However, I don't know the current congregation or its leadership, and I don't wish to cast aspersions in that direction.

The "old shul" is based on the Orthodox congregation my grandparents attended—but to simplify for the reader I made it a Reform shul and the early home of Shomrei Torah.

As I'm sure many people do, I regret not asking for more details of my parents' and grandparents' early lives while I could. So I've recreated old Trenton, and its Jewtown neighborhood, from my few memories and the details and photos I've found online. Like Steve's mother, my mother belonged to a social club sponsored by Har Sinai, called the Twenty-Thirty Club, though I don't believe she did any of the things that Sylvia Gordon did.

Steve shares his last name with my great-grandmother, Celia Levitan Kobrin, so I've always been conscious of his Jewish heritage, and I was eager to fit out this plot as a way for him to explore both his religion and his connection to Trenton. He's a good bit younger than I am, though, so I couldn't give him any of my early memories of that neighborhood by the river before it fell prey to urban renewal. My great-uncle, Louis Kobrin, did own a junkyard like the one in the book, though to my knowledge no murders occurred there or in its environs.

As always, thanks go to my critique group members: Christine Jackson, Kris Montee and Sharon Potts, whose help has been invaluable. My editor, Ramona de Felice Long, does a terrific job of helping me flesh out the characters and pointing out my errors – though any that remain are of course my own fault.

My golden retrievers, Brody and Griffin, are blessings to me every day – even when they get into trouble!

The Series

The Golden Retriever Mysteries, in order, are:

1: In Dog We Trust

2: The Kingdom of Dog 3: Dog Helps Those

4: Dog Bless You

5: Whom Dog Hath Joined 6: Dog Have Mercy

7: Honest to Dog

8: Dog is in the Details

9: Dog Knows

10: Dog's Green Earth

11: A Litter of Golden Mysteries (short stories)

12: Dog Willing

13: Dog's Waiting Room

14: Dog's Honest Truth

All are available in print, audio and e-book format, wherever books are sold.

Several short stories have also been published in the following anthologies:

"Dog Forbid," is featured in *Happy Homicides*. Interesting fact: the story in the ebook edition is set at Thanksgiving, but the editors wanted only Christmas stories for the paperback, so voila! the holiday was changed. Steve, Lili and Rochester accompany Mark, Joey and Brody to Pennsylvania Dutch Country, and suddenly Brody disappears. Can Rochester find him in time for a happy holiday?

Happy Homicides 2 is set at Valentine's Day and includes my story For the Love of Dog." While Gail's cafe, The Chocolate Ear, is being expanded into the space next door, a young woman's body is discovered there. It's up to Steve and Rochester to find out whodunnit.

The stories in *Happy Homicides 5* involve cats and crime—so a feline leads Rochester into an investigation of kidnapping and bitcoin fraud in "Riding the Tiger."

Thanks for reading! I hope you will visit my website at www.mahubooks.com where you can sign up for my golden retriever newsletter and see the other books I've written. Also follow me on Facebook, Twitter, Instagram and BookBub to hear about forthcoming books.

About the Author

Neil Plakcy's golden retriever mysteries have been inspired by his own goldens, Samwise, Brody and Griffin. A native of Bucks County, PA, where the books are set, Neil is a graduate of the University of Pennsylvania, Columbia University and Florida International University, where he received his MFA in creative writing.

He has written and edited many other books; details can be found at his website, http://www.mahubooks.com. Neil, his partner, Brody and Griffin live in South Florida, where Neil is writing and the dogs are undoubtedly getting into mischief.

www.ingramcontent.com/pod-product-compliance
Lightning Source LLC
LaVergne TN
LVHW012015060526
838201LV00061B/4314